MUMBLINGS

West Virginia Horror Stories

CAITLYN PACE

Illustrations By
KAITLYN TAYLOR

The Henlo Press

PRINTED IN THE UNITED STATES OF AMERICA
FIRST PRINTING, 2021

ISBN-978-1-962019-05-7

THE HENLO PRESS
P.O. BOX 1694ASHLAND, KY 41105
WWW.THEHENLOPRESS.COM

CONTENTS

FOREWORD

As a child growing up in West Virginia, I used to ask my grandmother (who was raised in Point Pleasant, West Virginia) if she had ever seen the Mothman. As the years went on, I collected stories from family members, friends, and teachers regarding anything from their personal experiences in West Virginia to folklore they loved and was unique to the region.

While I was walking one day along the Carriage Trail in Charleston, West Virginia, I began to wonder: who exactly were the two women whose bodies were found while they were constructing the Carriage Trail? I put pen to paper and wrote "The Case of Emily Peter." For over a year, I compiled my own stories based off of the tales I had heard growing up.

I have decided to label my stories under the category of "Fictionettes," This is an original term meant to encase stories that are too long to be considered short stories and too short to be novellas. I sincerely hope that you enjoy my collection of fictionettes based off of folklore and other tales from West Virginia.

-Caitlyn Pace

DECAY OF BEAUTY

It was a Friday afternoon and Ruth and Hazel Ellis held their cardigans above their heads as they ran to the entrance of the Keith Albee Theatre. Hazel Ellis went by both names because she believed it sounded more elegant, like how everyone referred to Marilyn Monroe by both names. Most people didn't know that Ellis wasn't her last name. For those who knew that Ellis wasn't her last name and asked her why she went by both her first and middle name, Hazel Ellis always responded with, "Because Hollywood actresses need to have sophisticated names, but one should never reveal her last name to Hollywood." When asked why this was, Hazel Ellis never had an answer.

She wasn't a Hollywood actress yet, of course. As soon as she graduated from high school, Hazel Ellis planned to pack up all of her stuff, take her life's savings that she kept in a mason jar, and get on the next train to Hollywood. In the Keith Albee Theatre entrance, Hazel Ellis laughed the sort of laugh that showed she wasn't afraid to be loud. Let them turn and look. She continued to laugh as she and Ruth, whose name wasn't actually Ruth, wrung out their rain-soaked cardigans.

Ruth had gone by her grandmother's name ever since people told her that the resemblance was uncanny between her and her grandmother when her grandmother was her age. Ruth never laughed after her grandmother passed away four years ago, but she would occasionally smile a closed-lipped smile and touch her necklace with the three pearls at its center. It was the same necklace that her grandmother had worn her entire life until she died. Ruth gave such a smile at this moment.

The cardigans weren't fully dried, but they had stopped dripping puddles onto the floor as Hazel Ellis and Ruth walked up to the ticket booth.

Ruth traced her fingers along the black spider web-like imprint on the green marble that made up the ticket booth.

The curling iron that covered the windows opened up.

"Are you girls here for the show?" The ticket holder asked. His voice sounded like he was close to a coughing fit.

"Yes," Hazel Ellis responded. She leaned in closer and saw that the ticket holder's skin was pale gray. He had dark circles under his eyes and cracked, bleeding lips. His blue veins stuck out like bruises as he handed her the tickets.

"Thank you," Hazel Ellis mumbled, and she passed one of the tickets along to Ruth.

There are so few lovely places in this world. That is what Ruth's grandmother used to tell her whenever her mom complained about how ugly their hometown was becoming. Like most sayings from her grandmother, it was something that she tried to live by. There were very few beautiful places in this world, but the Keith Albee Theatre was one of them, and it was in her hometown.

The Keith Albee Theatre was the type of place that Hazel Ellis always overdressed for and still felt underdressed. It was also the type of place that commanded respect. A visitor never wanted to leave any particular area of the theatre for fear that her mind would fail to remember the details of the architecture. And so, Hazel Ellis looked along the walls while she and Ruth walked down the hallway, trying to find a flower, a curve of a line, or something that she had never seen before in all her time coming here as a young girl. As usual, Hazel Ellis found herself standing taller, holding her head up higher, as they continued to walk. With such an added height, Hazel Ellis was reminded of why she respected this place.

Hazel Ellis held the door open for Ruth as they walked into the showroom. Their two seats were in the middle of the room, and as they took them, the girls' eyes wandered over the golden frame outlining the stage. Two golden ladies perched on top of the frame, and a crown adorned its center. The curtain draped down from the ladies. Only minutes of observation had passed for the two girls before the show had begun.

It started with the tapping of a foot that echoed around the room. As the curtain rose, Ruth and Hazel Ellis saw the silhouette of a man. His bare feet shuffled across the floor as he pushed himself up, twisting in the air and landing. As he did, many of the other dancers – the girls couldn't count them all, but there were at least thirty of them – walked out in lines around him. They held their arms to make crescent shapes around their heads. There was no music, only the tapping of their feet.

Their arms fell back to their sides, without deliberation, while they shuffled forward. They leaned back and swayed their arms up into the air once more.

Hazel Ellis gripped the edge of her seat. Ruth reached up, and wrapped her hand around her pearl necklace.

The dancers at the edge of the stage ran forward and jumped into the air. Others followed behind them with similar movements. They all landed on their feet until the dancer in the center jumped. He spiraled in the air, and as he landed, there was a brief moment when he was on his feet, but his ankle bent. The crack reverberated around the room, and nausea crawled up Ruth's neck. When he cried out, she turned away. Hazel Ellis was still staring at the stage, her knuckles turning white around the bottom of the chair.

"I need to go to the bathroom," Ruth said, and Hazel Ellis nodded. They left the room while the rest of the audience was still staring at the closing curtains.

The women's bathroom was downstairs, and as they walked to it, neither of the girls said anything. They opened the bathroom door while staring at the ground, so they only saw the shoes first. Dark red shoes that had small heels at the back. Her dress was a lighter shade of red, cuffed just below her knees. It forgave all of the lines of her body to frame a square around her torso. She was only steps away from Ruth and Hazel Ellis, yet she didn't move.

Hazel Ellis was the one who saw her face first, and when she did, she grabbed Ruth's hand. Her eyes were two bloody clumps.

While her body remained still, her head moved back and forth, up and down, repeating the movements faster each time.

Ruth reached up her hand, and as her grip tightened, she felt the pearls fall around her.

As they clattered to the ground, the lady vanished in the blink of an eye as though she had never been there at all.

Ruth fell to the ground. She breathed heavily as she gathered the broken bits of the necklace into her hands. Hazel Ellis crouched beside her and began picking up the pearls into her own hands. Her only thought was, *The necklace was so beautiful for so long. It's such a shame. It will never be beautiful again with all of its broken pieces.*

THE SOULS LEAVE THE BODY
AFTER DEATH

"It died this morning," Mary cried while rubbing her fists against her eyes. "It sang to me every morning. I loved its music. It made me smile. Now, I will have nothing to smile about."

When I looked up at her, she stared down at the floor. She wiped her hand against her eyes, and her hand fell limply back at her side.

"Well, I'm very sorry to hear that, Mary, but your bird is in Heaven now. Some day, much further away from now, you will join your bird there too."

"I hope it's sooner than further away."

I reached up and grabbed onto her arm.

"Don't say that. Life is precious."

Mary didn't respond. She just sniffed and wiped another tear away before it could fall. "Would it make you happy if I buried your bird for you?" Her little head nodded a couple of times, and for once, she looked directly at me. "Then I will be sure to do that."

She wrapped her arms around me.

"You're a kind man," she said.

"Well, I try to be," I laughed. She turned her head to look up at me.

"Will you bring some dirt back in a handkerchief from the burial?"

"I'll be sure to do that," I said and patted her head.

She went to the bird lying on the ground. It looked like a pile of dirt in her hands as she scooped it up. She held it out before me and dropped it into my hands.

I could feel its bones against its skin and tried to tell myself it wasn't an animal, only rocks. That was what it felt like. I kept my gaze ahead.

"I'll be back with the dirt," I told Mary before I left her.

Carter had just planted new flowers out front. That was good because the dirt was still soft. I wouldn't have to find him to ask where they kept the shovels. I crouched down, scooped some dirt into my hands, and placed it to the side. It was a shallow hole. If the rain came, it would wash away the ground and the bird with it. I placed the bird inside the hole and sprinkled the dirt on top of it.

It was nothing more than a piece of cloth from my pocket. It was a shy excuse for a handkerchief, but it was the only thing resembling a handkerchief I had.

I pinched off a bit of the dirt covering the bird and put it in the cloth. Then, I broke off a flower petal from the plant the bird was buried underneath, and I put it on top of the dirt before I tied the ends of the cloth together.

When Mary saw me walking back, she started to run towards me. I held out a hand for her to slow down, but she reached me before she did. I dropped the cloth into her open hand.

"Buried it underneath some flowers."

She wrapped her arms around me again, and I returned the embrace.

"You are the kindest doctor here."

"Oh, I'm no doctor," I said. "Maybe one day, but I'm only a worker for now."

"I hope you stay a worker forever so you always stay kind."

"Now, there are kind doctors here." I pulled away. She shook her head.

"The doctors here say I am getting better, but I feel sicker."

"Well, maybe you should talk to them about that."

"It's okay. Thank you for this. I know you need to return to your work."

I nodded at her, but she didn't look up to see. She only stared at the cloth in her hands while she walked away.

When I walked by, the few patients in the hallways kept their gazes towards the ground. I turned the corner and opened the door. The air was warmer outside with the afternoon sun. Carter was sitting on a bench, eating his own meal. When I saw him, he looked up at me.

"Oh, I need to tell you something," he yelled as I started to walk towards him.

"Good afternoon, Carter."

"Now," he said and pointed a finger at me. "I have an opportunity for you."

"And what is that?" I sat down on the bench beside him. I unwrapped the cloth around my food.

"You need to deliver two bodies up to Graham Hamrick in Philippi. He lives on a farm. Ask around town and they'll tell you where he is once you get there. The cart with the bodies is outside, in front of the building."

I tore off a corner of a piece of bread and put it in my mouth. "Two bodies from here?"

"Yes, two female patients, dead and gone. I don't know when they died, though. It certainly wasn't today."

"Why does Hamrick need two bodies?"

"He's making this potion, I suppose, to turn dead people into mummies. Says he's already mummified fruits and vegetables and small animals with it. Wants to see if he can mummify a human now."

"And why would we let him see?"

"Why wouldn't we let him?"

I dropped my food onto the cloth spread across my legs and stared directly at him. "Those are two girls," I said. "They have families who would wonder—"

"Their families don't care anything about them. I'm willing to bet those girls have been here for most of their lives. After a year, if there's no letter from a family member, they've forgotten about the person. They might have put them up here to forget about them. They don't care about whether or not they lived or died or what anyone did with the body after they died. When a person walks through the doors of this place, they're already dead to most everyone who knows them."

"There are some people who still care about the patients here."

"The doctors and staff, maybe. Perhaps some people on the outside still do, but most people out there are living their lives. They don't care about the patients here, even if they are their families."

"Well, even if they have no family who wants to have a funeral for them, they still deserve to be buried. They were people, too; they deserve anything anybody else gets."

"Yes, they were people and got what most people get in this place. For now, though, what used to make them people is up in Heaven or Hell. I hope it's Heaven for their sakes, but their bodies are just bodies now. It doesn't matter what happens to them. People only bury the dead for the living."

"And what if they're looking down at us from Heaven and they see us disrespecting their bodies?"

"I don't think it's any less disrespectful to give the bodies to a man for his experiments than it is to bury bodies in unmarked graves, which is where their bodies would end up if you don't deliver them to Mr. Hamrick."

"I don't think it's right."

"Well, there's already been an official document drafted and everything. The bodies are legally his."

"Is there not someone else who could take them?"

Carter stood up and sighed. "They are going to be delivered, whether you deliver them or not," he said and patted me on the shoulder before he walked away.

I heard the horses first – neighing and stumbling about as if there was about to be a thunderstorm - before I saw them.

They were attached to the cart, and a blanket lay beside them. *Why not finish the job and cover them up?* I thought, and I forced myself to move forward.

The smell of rot and decay filled my nostrils. I took out the cloth my food had been wrapped in and held it to my nose. Their mouths were open, and gnats crawled around them before flying away. Their gray skin wrapped around their protruding bones, and one of the girls still had her eyes open. They were the gray color of a corpse. I had only ever seen that color when both of my grandparents passed away.

I grabbed the blanket. If a patient were to look out of the window and see this...

"Goodbye," I said through the cloth. "I hope you've reached Heaven, and I hope it's better than here."

As I was about to put the blanket over them, I saw a white square extending out of one of their dresses. I leaned over the cart while swatting the flies away and tried to only breathe through my mouth as I picked up the paper.

The letter was folded about four or six times. I unfolded it carefully, preventing myself from tearing it in one movement.

Weston WV 188-

Dear Brother, I take my pen in hand to write to you to inform you I am well at present and hope those few lines find you well. I quit taking medicine and feel better than when I was taken. I have been thinking of coming home for some time, but the doctors still say it is better to stay put. I believe that I am as well as I will ever get. I suppose my husband is at your house if he is you can give him the letter to read as I have never received any from him since I have been here. I will come home as soon as he comes after me, and the Lord being willing, I hope that will be soon. Give my love to all inquiring friends. No more at present.

    Love, L Warner.

I turned the paper over.

Mrs. Warner is doing well. Her general health is good. Mentally she is improving.

    Respectfully,

    WJ. Blaney.

The letter was addressed to Mr. John L. Pfan, Philippi, Barbour County, West Virginia.

I wiped the tears away that fell from my eyes and mumbled, "I am so sorry," to both of them. I leaned forward and tucked the letter into her pocket, all folded once more. I then took the blanket and covered them up.

The horses' hooves clattered against the road. I kept waiting for people to stop and stare, but they only made passing glances at me. Perhaps the stench wasn't as horrendous a few steps away from the cart.

More than once, I thought about stopping and burying them on the side of the road. Each of them would have a little cross made of fallen branches and grass to tie the branches together, like Alice had shown me how to make when we were younger.

I only ever thought about it, though, as the horses continued moving forward. But Alice, thinking of her was enough to bring some peace to my being.

I remembered when we ran out to the fields last summer, and we were laughing, and the sun embraced her skin. She held onto my hands, and we spun around together like children. Her white gown fluttered up and around her and looked like wings. We were a lot younger then.

When the season passed, I would see her again. If she would have me, I would never leave her again.

Occasionally, I would have to tug on the ropes to guide the horses. Each movement reminded me that I was dragging the girls forward as if they deserved the fate they were about to receive. A small sign on the side of the road marked the town of Philippi. The sun was beginning to set, and a few people outside walked back to what I presumed were their homes. Although, I couldn't see any buildings from where I was.

"Excuse me, sir," I said to a man walking by. He was short and had dirt and sweat covering his face and staining his shirt. He stopped walking when he saw me.

"Yes, sir?"

"Do you happen to know where Graham Hamrick's farm is?"

"Well, yes, it's up that way," He said while pointing to a direction forward along the road. "Take a right; you will see nothing but rolling hills for a while. Continue, even when you think you've been continuing for too long, and the house should be at the end of the dirt pathway. There's a lake along the way up there for your horses to get some water from."

"Well, thank you," I said.

"If I may ask, what are you bringing to Mr. Hamrick exactly?"

I paused for a moment before I said, "A delivery from the state mental hospital," I said, like the bodies were nothing more than food or clothes. I started my horses forward.

～

The sky was the shade of ashes and blush, and the sun peaked above the mountains when I came across the lake. I pulled my horses to the side and got out of the cart. I unhooked them and walked them to the lake, tying them to a nearby tree. As they drank, I leaned against the tree and watched the sunset.

I could stay here for the night. There could be dangers on the road until the sun rises again. Even as I had the thought, I knew that the danger I would most likely come across would be nothing more than a deer walking across the road at night. It was already so quiet; I could hear a squirrel drop an acorn from the top of a tree. I would surely be able to hear everything else.

The bodies will be delivered, whether I do it myself or someone else does.

When the horses were finished, I untied the ropes from the tree and walked them back over to the cart.

The warm candlelight in the window flickered brighter than the stars piercing through the sky. I brought my horses to a still in front of the house, made my way to the door, and knocked.

Graham Hamrick answered. I knew it was him even before he said his name because as soon as he opened the door, I could smell the decay from inside his house.

I thought I had gotten used to stenches from working at the mental hospital. People were sometimes one step away from decaying there, but here, the smell of rotten eggs seemed to cling to my nose in the muggy air.

"Hello," I stumbled over the sounds of the letters while I tried to pronounce them. "Um, are you Graham Hamrick?"

"I sure am."

"Well, I'm one of the workers at the mental institution in Weston. I have the two bodies you requested."

We stared at each other for a good while. I turned my head

down, only returning my gaze up when I heard Mr. Hamrick start to laugh.

He had one hand wrapped across his stomach and the other on the doorframe to keep himself from falling over.

"Well, they sure don't deliver bodies by mail, do they?" He said once he had regained himself. "Now, come on in."

Even though I was nauseous, I held my breath and stepped through the door.

"I am mighty grateful to you for bringing those bodies to me. I had no semblance of an idea of how I would get the bodies to begin with, never mind being able to have them delivered to my property. I am very grateful to you for doing that. You can stay the night here if you would like. It's the least I can offer you. Are you hungry?"

I declined.

"Well, if you do become hungry, I have some bread here," he said while we walked into the kitchen. "And I have some meat and wine in here." He gestured in different directions, of which I only saw in the edges of my vision while I watched him. "You can help yourself to any of it."

"Perhaps later," I said.

His eyebrows pinched together, and he tried to make eye contact with me. I turned my head down to stare at the ground.

Then, he finally let out a breath of understanding. "I know what it is," he said. "You're not accustomed to the smell. It took me quite a long time to get accustomed to myself, but I'm afraid you won't be here long enough for it to smell any different to you. If it becomes too much for you to handle, you can leave. I would advise against that, though. The roads aren't safe during this time of the night."

"Do you believe in God?"

Mr. Hamrick's lips moved, but no words came from them until he stammered, "More or less."

"Well, if you do, even in the least bit, do you think what you're about to do to those two girls is wrong?"

The corners of his lips turned down. "Correct me if I am wrong, but I believe they are both dead."

"They are, but does that change anything?"

"Not necessarily, no," he said, leaning back slightly. "The same is true, though. I do not believe what I am doing is wrong. I could stand here and explain why I think so, or I could show you. I much prefer that option. Follow me, if you will."

I shook my head, but he continued to stare at me. His gaze felt like when I was six years old, and my skin had turned red and blistered from being out in the sun for too long. In the pit of my stomach, I knew that the only way I could get rid of the feeling was if I followed him, satisfied him, so he would leave me be.

He led me to a room whose door he had to unlock with a key he pulled out of his pocket. As the door opened, the smell of whatever was inside made my eyes water. I fumbled with a cloth from my pocket, pulled it out, and held it up to my nose and mouth.

"Now, look around and tell me what you see," Mr. Hamrick said.

It appeared as nothing more than dead leaves clumped together at first, but when I picked it up, it held together. Its skin was wasted away to a dark brown and thin enough for me to rip it apart by hardly moving my finger across it, but it still held the shape of an apple. Beside it were strings of green beans that had the same texture and appearance as leather.

I looked at the table beside it. Thin, hairless skin stretched over brittle bones. Their eyes were a cloudy gray, but they seemed to look into me. Their nails protruded from their frail fingers, and the pointed ends seemed to claw into their palms. Their mouths were held agape, as if to give a final cry. My skin started to itch, and I turned away. There were at least five decaying animals on that table. Around them were bottles of liquid in various shades of green. It was almost like lake water.

The tables themselves had dark stains forming around fresh blood puddles that reflected against the candlelight. A long, pink thing wrapped around itself near the pools. I thought it was some type of worm or insect until I realized it was part of an intestine. The paws of an animal, detached and stripped of fur, lay next to the intestine. It was still a light pink color, not yet having begun to rot.

"What do you see?" Mr. Hamrick repeated his question.

I stared at the ground as I muttered, "Nothing but death and decay."

"Death, yes, I agree with you on that point, but not decay. What if I told you that every single thing in this room died at least three months ago?"

I remained silent as Mr. Hamrick continued.

"Well, they would have decayed a lot more now, would they have not? I have simply preserved them, so they may escape the look of death that we all despise to one day have."

I was unable to meet Mr. Hamrick's gaze, but I nodded.

"These things had little to no meaning before I started my experiment on them. Now, they will exist for eternity. Such a long existence that is nothing that life could ever offer. In that way, I have not taken anything away from these things, and I will not be taking anything away from those two girls. I will be allowing them to become something more than they would have ever been able to become, and how could something such as this be wrong? I am giving more meaning to their lives, after all."

Amid the silence, he said. "Well, at least, that is what I believe." He started to make his way out of the room. "The smell's starting to get to me too."

❧

On the ground near the kitchen, with nothing more than a blanket, sleep never came to me that night. When I saw the first touch of light through the windowpane, I put on my shoes, grabbed a piece of bread from the kitchen, and left. It was colder than it had been during the night in the early morning air.

My cart was in front of the house. The bodies were already gone, and the blanket was folded and tucked into a back corner. I only looked away from the cart when I heard my horses neighing nearby. They were tied to a tree near the house.

I walked over to them and untied them. They seemed like they were about to buck any moment, but I held my hand up to the front of their faces. Once they knew it was me, their breathing started to slow until I could pull them forward without spooking them. I guided them over to the cart and secured everything. As soon as I sat down on the seat, my horses started walking forward without me having to urge them to do so. Turning around to give one last look at the farm, I whispered a silent prayer to myself.

NEXT TO THE SOUVENIR SHOP

The shadows flitted through the metal bars spanning across each side, like how the sunlight flickered across my hands on the drive here. But my thoughts weren't wandering here like they did in the car. My body and mind were rigid, like I was trying to move through sleep paralysis.

The lights from our phones trailed ahead of us, creating a gray fog. The musty smell of the decrepit building burned through my nostrils.

We were just by the souvenir shop. A long, red line was painted on the ground, only inches away from the right wall. The voice from the tour guide we had departed from an hour before echoed in my mind.

"This hallway is where the prisoners had to line up," he said and gestured for us to move behind the red line. Helen and Ally did, but I stood away with some of the other people from our group.

"Now, if any prisoner stepped past this red line, the corrections officer," the guide put his middle and pointer finger together. "Cha-boom," he shook his hand to mimic a gun going off.

A green radar was displayed across Helen's phone screen with tiny, white dots along each circle. Since we left the tour guide, we had all accepted that the little white dots were only dots, not the ghosts that the free app had claimed.

"Who's with us?" Helen asked into the phone.

Bicycle, it said across the screen. I squinted my eyes at the word, and Ally and Helen laughed.

"This app really doesn't know anything."

"Shh, you're going to scare off the ghosts," Ally said. Even in the shadows, I could see her smiling.

A wire cage wrapped around us at the entrance of the cells just below our heads. Within it, there were a few cells along with two cafeteria tables. I stopped in front of one of the tables. I felt my sister lean in beside me.

"Hey, do you remember what his name was?" She asked as she tilted her head towards the ground.

When our tour guide told us that there was an inmate who was stabbed here and had bled out on this floor, he pointed at a spot on the ground that remained in an unmoving shadow. As I stood on the spot, I saw that the floor was, indeed, darker than the area around it.

It can't be blood, I thought. *It would have washed away by now.* But I still stepped to the side.

Helen held her phone up to her mouth and asked, "Prisoner who was stabbed here, what is your name?'

Ally and I leaned in closer to the phone. I started pressing my thumb into the prints of each of my fingertips – pointer, middle, ring, pinky, pointer, middle – but the minutes passed, and the screen remained blank.

I watched until the time reached 11:25 before I pulled myself away and left Ally and Helen to themselves.

As I walked down the hallway, I glanced into each cell. The walls were covered in red and black spray-painted slurs, Bible verses, and swastikas.

I blinked, and the world around me felt like I had just woken up. Chills spread across my shoulders as I heard Ally yelling out my name.

Her running footsteps rattled the metal cage that continued over the cells where I was standing. I pointed my flashlight at her, and she lifted her arm to shield her eyes.

As she dropped her arm back down and held her phone out in a trembling hand, I saw her eyes glistening. I grabbed onto the phone.

The screen displayed *Mark.*

"His name was Mark," Ally called out as she ran up to us.

"Yeah," I said. "But maybe it wasn't."

"What?"

"That's the only logical response we've gotten all night."

"Yeah, so maybe it's just saying random words. It's probably just a coincidence that it said a name now."

Helen reached up to grab her phone back when I saw that the word had changed to *Left*.

"See," I said. "It's just saying random words."

"Left," Helen mumbled.

"We should follow it," I suggested. "It probably doesn't lead anywhere anyway. Nothing to be scared about."

"I don't know," Helen said.

"Yeah, we should. I don't think it will lead us nowhere, but maybe it will show us someplace we haven't been to yet." I said.

"No, I'm not going to any place our tour guide didn't show us."Ally said.

"Let's follow it," I said and turned to Helen. "But if you start getting freaked out, let us know, and we'll turn around."

She stared at me with wide eyes.

"Here, do you want me to take the phone?" Ally asked, and Helen briefly nodded. I stayed by my sister's side. The word remained on the screen. We walked past the cage into another with cells on one side and a wall on the other.

The word changed to *Right*.

"This doesn't seem random anymore," Helen mumbled while we all turned right.

"It's -" I started to say before Ally cut me off.

"We were just here," she whined.

I saw the red line first, going down the hallway as far as I could see. It was right next to the door that led to the souvenir shop.

"Cha-boom," the tour guide's voice echoed through my mind.

"The phone's just tracking our movements," I muttered, barely lifting my gaze off the red line.

Helen shook her head. "Look," she whispered.

I leaned in to look at the top of the phone screen that Helen was pointing at. The time read 12:00 AM.

"It was eleven-thirty. It didn't take us a half hour to get here."

Ally started walking towards the door. "Well, it's good that we followed it, or else our tour guide would have had to come looking for us."

Bicycle. I saw the word appear on the screen before Helen turned off the phone.

Ally held open the door for us as we walked back into the souvenir shop.

I made my way over to the display case of books. *History of Moundsville State Penitentiary* was the title. I picked it up and carried it to the register.

I pushed the book over the counter, and the woman operating the register ran it through. Pennies from my wallet clattered onto the counter while she told me my total. I tried to scoop them all back into my hand. When I grabbed the bag, she smiled at me, and I smiled back. Helen and Ally waved goodbye to our tour guide and a few others standing with him.

"What did you get?" My sister asked me while Helen opened the door for us to leave the building.

"A book."

"Of course you would," she said. "What's it about?"

"The history of the prison."

I grabbed my water bottle with one hand and the car door handle with the other. I took a drink and fell into the back seat. The book lazily dangled from my grasp on the handle of the plastic bag. I adjusted my seat belt and then brought out the book.

Most of the pages had only pictures with small captions beside them. Helen started driving, and I saw glimpses of them as we passed by street lamps.

We passed one of them, and I stopped flipping through the pages at a bronze circle.

I grabbed my phone from my pocket and turned on the flashlight. When I saw it, my fingernails pressed into the pages until they bent backward.

"What is it?" Ally asked.

I lifted one finger up to point at the page. She squinted until her eyes adjusted to the brightness of the flashlight.

"Oh my God," she let out each word in one breath as she read the line underneath the pictures of men standing beside their creations in an assembly line: "Pictured above: Prisoners Mark Salisbury, Alexander Kirk, and Landon Parrish are in the process of creating bicycles as part of their prison labor." Beside them was the red line painted across the door I had walked across into the souvenir shop.

MUMBLINGS

Peter was the one driving. He was always the one driving, even though Lucile tried to take the keys from him before they got into the car. He liked to dangle the keys in front of her and then drop them into his hand as if to say, "you're too slow."

It was nearing midnight. The speedometer edged close to eighty. There were no lights on the backwoods roads in Harper's Ferry. Their only guide was the car's headlights. Forests surrounded them on all sides. If they had turned off the car, Lucile wouldn't have been able to see her hand in front of her face.

They hit a bump in the road. The sides of the car started shaking, but Peter continued driving as if there was nothing there. Lucile found the indenture of the scar on the side of her cheek and traced over it.

"Shouldn't you slow down?" She asked.

"Come on, do you want to get back home before the sun rises or not?"

Lucile pressed her lips tightly against one another. She dropped her hand by her side and began to twist at the skin on her left ring finger.

There were a thousand mumblings in the back of her throat that remained there.

Three months ago, he put a ring on her finger, and they were engaged, just like that. Engaged is a funny word. If "engaged" were an abstract image, it would be one of a child trying to fit shapes into her cutout board. A rhombus goes into a rhombus cutout, a square goes into a square cutout, and on it goes. Of course, a young child who is still learning the names of shapes doesn't know that, so she puts a rhombus in a circle and then tries it in the square, taking them out and forcing them into the cutouts until they fit. Somehow, it just all works out.

The thought of children always made the back of Lucile's throat close. She didn't think she could have children. There was no question about her fertility. Her mom made sure that she was checked to see if she could have babies as soon as she told her of the engagement.

"One day, you're going to marry a great man, and you'll have lots of children. Those children will be my grandchildren, and you'll make me very happy." Lucile's mother told her this all throughout her childhood. Usually, after her mother said this, Lucile would point at the scars all over her face. When she was a child, those scars were still red and puckered. She responded, "Nobody wants to marry someone with my face." That's what the girls at school had told her, and she believed them for the longest time. She was a stupid child.

Her mom would then hug her and say, "Love overcomes all. Your husband will truly love you, and he'll love everything about you, including your scars."

Her mom had been right about some things.

That was why she had thought Peter loved her. He would kiss her without flinching and look directly into her eyes instead of staring at her scars like other people did. He never mentioned anything about her being unattractive, even during his hateful moments. Well, not directly, anyhow.

Her fingers rested against her stomach. She imagined it growing until it was round to hold her child. Peter's child. She imagined pushing the child out of her and then holding the baby close to her chest. So new to this world, so innocent.

It wasn't right to bring a child into this world. There were too many broken places for them to fall into, too many scars to develop.

But Lucile would have a baby. She would probably have several because her mother wanted her to. Her mother hadn't smiled in years, not since her hand slipped from the steering wheel. She always made Lucile smile, though, nearly every day. She wanted to see her mom smile again. She owed that to her.

The wind whipped past the car.

"Jesus, how fast are you going?"

"Don't worry about it."

"Tell me!"

"I said don't worry about it," Peter's voice was still calm, even as the heat rose into Lucy's cheeks.

"Slow down! If you can't talk, then do that, at least."

"Don't talk to me like that. I know what I'm doing."

"You're wrong."

"What did you say?"

"Slow down."

Peter pushed on the accelerator even more.

"How fucking fast are you going now?" Sometimes, these little mumblings would slip out.

"Watch your mouth, woman. I'm going however fucking fast I want to go. We're in the middle of nowhere. It's not like we're going to hit somebody."

Lucile leaned further back into her seat.

"I'm sorry," she said.

"You should be."

Lucile pressed her lips tightly against one another and traced the scar at the corner of her eye. "I don't like it. You knew our car was going fast when we crashed or did you forget about that already?"

"What? The car crash that happened when you were six? Jesus, Lucy, you should be over that by now. I'm surprised you even remember it. I can't remember anything from my childhood."

Lucile looked out at the darkness around her. The silence was deafening, but it was also relieving.

She hated when Peter called her Lucy. She liked her full name, Lucile. It was elegant and light, and she liked how her lips formed the sounds of the word.

Her lips curved over the letters in her name, which she was careful to whisper, when she was cut off by a sudden gasp that remained as a choke in the back of her throat. Two red dots - *what were they?* - burned into the corner of her right eye. She tried to convince herself that the two red dots were nothing more than lights in the distance, but her gut knew that it was not.

Then the dots were in front of the car.

"Goddammit!" Peter screamed. He slammed the breaks, but he had been going too fast. The car rolled over the dots and there was a crunch of impact. The car bounced overtop of whatever it was and came to a stop. Peter smacked his open palms against the steering wheel. "There wasn't supposed to be anything on this street!"

"What did you hit?" Lucile whispered the question. She pressed her hand into her chest, but it didn't help her heartbeat to slow down.

"Some type of animal. I think it was a dog. It was black as night, though. Wouldn't have been able to see it if I had been driving slower."

There was a click as Peter opened his door.

"Don't go out there."

Peter had one foot already out of the car. He turned back slowly to face Lucile. "What did you say?"

"Don't go out there," Lucile said as her voice rose. "What if it's feral? It could attack you."

"I need to see how much damage it caused to the damn car, and if it's still alive," he said more to himself, "it could be hurt."

He had the courtesy to close the door as soon as he left the car. *Always a gentleman on the outside,* Lucile thought. The pounding in her head began to leave her.

She rubbed her fingers into the scar on her cheek. The car could've flipped over when Peter had hit whatever he had just hit. She thought of their bodies lying there, upside down in their seats, and her finger pressed into her cheek so hard that she could feel the inside rubbing against her teeth.

"There's nothing there," Peter said as she started to get back into the car.

"What?"

"There's nothing there. Not even a scratch or a dent in the car, so before you say anything about driving slower, think better of it because there was no harm done."

It would have been better to drive slower, though. It was always better to go slower. She always knew what was better to do. Peter always made the mistakes, even though he would disagree. Deep down, though, she knew she made the better choices. As a consequence, she knew she was better than Peter. It was what kept her from doubting herself whenever Peter talked to her like she was nothing.

She knew so much more than he ever would. She was the one who had gotten a full ride to a college out of state when Peter had barely gotten into community college. He had dragged her to community college with him. He had said that, if she had gone to the out-of-state college and had only visited him on breaks, he would be so lonely that he would have to seek comfort in the other girls around him. At that time, she still believed that he was the only man who would want to marry her.

How stupid she had been. She hadn't always known more than Peter, after all.

She had graduated early and immediately started her internship at the radio station. He dropped out at the end of the fourth year and told her he had found a job repairing cars. He never came home dirty or smelled of gasoline or motor oil.

Perhaps there were things that both Peter and Lucile didn't know about each other.

"Why are you so quiet? It's like I'm driving alone."

"Don't you like that?"

"If I liked it, then I would drive alone. Come on, what are you thinking about? You must be thinking about something, with you being so quiet and all."

"I'm just thinking."

"Jesus Christ, Lucy, I need something to distract myself from what just happened."

"Why don't you slow down, then? I know it will calm your nerves."

Peter snickered. "You always think you know best."

"I do know best."

Peter pushed his foot further down onto the gas pedal. The wind speeding past them sounded like the start of a thunderstorm.

"Peter, what are you doing?"

He shrugged. "I only want to get home faster. I hate driving when I feel like I'm alone."

"Then turn on the goddamn radio."

Peter only laughed. Lucile reached up to turn on the radio. As the distant station started to play a song, the sound was barely distinguishable from that of a broken record.

"Turn that off, Lucy."

"Then slow down the goddamn car."

"Turn it off."

"SLOW DOWN THE CAR."

Peter pushed his foot further down onto the gas pedal.

"I want out."

"What? I can't hear you over the radio."

"I WANT OUT OF THIS CAR RIGHT NOW! LET ME OUT!"

Peter turned off the radio. He pulled his foot off of the gas and slammed the brakes. His head whipped forward, and the sudden stop pushed him hard against the chair.

"Suit yourself," he said.

Tears stung the backs of Lucile's eyes. She pushed at her seatbelt until it was undone, opened her car door, and stepped out.

The wind stung her bare arms. She crossed them over her chest and marched forward. Her brain was fuzzy, and her cheeks were warm.

The car rumbled across the road as it slowly approached her.

"Are you being serious, Lucy?"

She didn't respond.

Peter started laughing.

She turned to look at him. It was the same laugh he had whenever she tried to ask him where he had been all day.

"Good times," he would always say after that laugh.

It was the same laugh he had when their friends at the dinner party congratulated them on their engagement.

It really was all just one big joke to him.

"Come on, Lucy, get back in the car. You're acting like a goddamn child."

"Funny you should say that," Lucile growled underneath her breath.

"What?"

But Lucile continued to walk forward as the car inched towards her.

"Lucy, I'm going to ask you one more time, or—"

"Or you'll what? Drag me back into the car?" She scoffed. "I'd like to see you try. Maybe you'll leave me out here until another guy picks me up." She tapped her pointer finger against the side of her lips like she was deciding something. "I wonder what types of guys I'll meet here."

Peter's knuckles were white from gripping onto the steering wheel. "This is not the woman I chose to marry," he said.

"Well," Lucile threw her hands up into the air before she turned around and stuck them and her head through the car window. "I guess you won't be marrying me, then."

Peter was breathing heavily, but he kept his lips shut. "What do you mean by that?" He paused at the end of each word.

"Oh, you know," Lucile started. She drew invisible circles on her arm with her finger.

"What?"

"How I got that position at the radio station? I met someone there. He treats me real nice. I'm not going to tell you his name. I don't want you to go finding him and all, but he treats me better than you have or ever could."

"Shut up."

"I don't mean by buying me things. I couldn't care less about that. He really understands me. He respects me more than anybody else in my life has before." When Lucile looked directly at Peter, she saw that he was looking past her shoulder instead of at her.

"Lucy, get into the car."

"Why?"

Peter dropped one hand from the steering wheel and clenched it into a fist. He leaned in closer to Lucile. "Look, we'll talk about this later. Get into the car right now."

Lucile opened the car door. For a second, she hesitated. Then, she closed the door until it was only an inch open. *Remember your manners,* her mom's voice rang in the back of her head.

The voice was enough to make heat rise into her chest, but she found herself abiding the words.

"You're not going to speed again, are you?" She asked.

Fallen branches started to snap behind her.

"Lucile, get into this goddamn car right now. I think there's something behind you."

Lucile opened the door further, but she turned to look behind her before she stepped in.

There were two red, glowing orbs in the darkness. They were slightly higher than her waist and only a few steps away. A low growl sounded from amid the trees.

Lucile slammed the car door shut behind her. Peter stepped onto the gas while she struggled to put on her seatbelt.

"PETER, SLOW DOWN!"

That same damn laugh.

"What are you going to do? Step out of the car again? No, I won't let you, not this time."

Her heartbeat wrapped around her neck. She finished securing her seatbelt, and from the corner of her eye, she could see Peter shake his head.

"I can't believe you're leaving me over some lousy guy at a radio station. He probably doesn't even love you, you know. He just sees you as an easy target."

"I thought we were going to talk about this when we got home." Lucile put her head in her hands. "Jesus Christ, Peter, slow down."

"Oh, so would you rather be eaten by the animal that's been following us?"

"I would rather us not get into a car crash." Lucile paused. "How do you know it's been following us?"

"I swear it's the same thing I hit earlier. I just have this feeling."

"Slow down. It can't get us as long as we're moving in this car."

"You don't know that, Lucy. You think that you know so much, but you don't-"

"PETER, WATCH OUT!"

In the car's headlights, Peter and Lucile saw the animal on all fours. Its fur was hardly distinguishable from the night. Its red, burning eyes turned to look at them as Peter swerved and drove head-on into a cluster of trees.

The police looked at the mangled bodies in the car's front seats. The shattered glass from the windshield pierced their skin like thorns on the stems of roses. Blood, dried so that it almost appeared black, oozed from the tops of their heads, down their necks. The one in the front driver's seat still had his eyes open, and they were a dull gray. The woman, only noticeable by her torn dress, had her eyes closed like she had expected to die all along and didn't want to watch. But her mouth was open, perhaps held in a scream. It was no wonder; whatever had gotten to them had taken the most bites out of her. They had chunks of skin torn out across their bodies, but mostly their arms and legs. The police officers could see the yellow, puffy fat and layers of muscle underneath the bite marks.

"It really was as bad as they said." The police officer shook his head.

"I wonder what could have caused this?"

He shrugged. "It could have been a number of things: drugs, alcohol."

One of the officers shone a flashlight into the car. "Hey, come look at this." The other officer walked up to where he was standing. "You see how bits of their skin are missing in chunks?"

"Yeah, some animal must've gotten to them. Hey," he said and hit the other officer against the back, "maybe it was the Snarly Yow." He broke out into laughter, but the other officer could only manage a smile.

When the laughter died, he said, "Let's call in some backup. We'll need to have this wreck cleaned up before people start their morning commutes."

THE CASE OF EMILY PETER

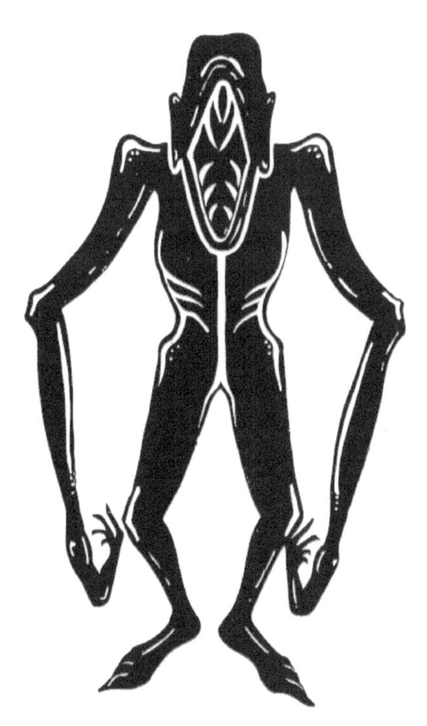

| Charles Investigative Company |
Charleston, West Virginia

Notes:

June 12, 2021

The team and I at Charles Investigative Company have been working on the Emily Peter case for over a year. We were assigned to this particular case through the missing person's family, two weeks after her disappearance was reported. We have completed extensive investigations and research into this case, the details of which are in the case files at the Charles Investigative Company. However, our efforts have not drawn us any closer to where Emily Peter may be.

Emily Peter is a writer best known for her horror novel, *Lock and I Will Open*. A successful young author with many best-selling stories, Emily Peter kept a journal where she extensively outlined her daily habits and rituals.

We found th is journal shortly after the family hired us for the case. We went through all of Emily Peter's possessions in the cabin she stayed in during the personal writing retreats she took in West Virginia each year. **

In her journal, Peter would often use word choices and incorrect grammar that did not line up with her professional writing. This suggests to me that her journal was entirely personal and she did not plan to share it with anyone.

It is my belief that we are overlooking an important aspect among our research and previous investigations and have decided to once again read over and analyze Emily Peter's journal entries from the time just before she went missing. It is my hope that this analysis will give us the break we need to progress further in this case.

** Emily Peter rented this same cabin from a local couple every year. They have asked to remain anonymous with any files that are not directly associated with their own personal interview and other statements, as many others have. They have been generous throughout the search, and they even donated to the Peter Family Foundation to help fund the investigation.

11-16-19

I'm staying in a cabin about 45 minutes outside of Charleston. It's a nice drive to the Carriage Trail everyday. I enjoy the time it takes to get there. It's time to think and to slow down. So many ideas, but none of them good ones.

My cabin is not supposed to have any distractions. I mean, it's quite literally in the middle of nowhere. But I guess that, when I don't have any ideas, I find distractions. I've been staring at the window and trying to make shapes out of the clouds recently. Sometimes I will even count the leaves on the tree just outside of the window that is in front of my writing desk. I spend all of my time when I'm not writing wanting to write, and when I sit down to write, none of it is good. I need to get out of my head more, but a wandering mind is as vital to the writing process as writing itself.

I always feel better and ready to write when I come home from the Carriage Trial. I feel like I am taking the same steps as someone a hundred years ago took. Funny how much a culture changes but how little a place can change.

Glimpses of the Carriage Trail that I can maybe use somewhere in a future writing project: two memorials stained with years of rain and weather. The first for the two women whose bodies were found when they were building the trail. The second, a statue of Christ for MacCorkle. I do not know if he is buried here or if it is just a remembrance for him. There is the imprint of leaves on the stones lining the trail, and moss covers the bridges. In the summer, the trail is full of birds chirping and blooming plants. In the autumn, I only ever hear ravens and crows. As the leaves fall from the trees, there is a mist that always seems to hang around that place.

| Charles Investigative Company |
Charleston, West Virginia

Notes:

While Emily Peter wrote many stories about hiking trails during the year of 2019, she never published or wrote any specific story about the Carriage Trail.

Several people have come forward and said that they saw Emily Peter taking daily walks on the Carriage Trail, usually between the hours of 3 and 5 in the evening. She would sometimes walk the trail four or five times, since it is not long.

We can confirm that the cabin Emily Peter stayed in was isolated, but she did have neighbors that lived within twenty minutes of her. The neighbors knew her, and they told us that they often invited her for dinner parties and lunches at their houses. While she accepted all of thei r offers, she never invited them to her cabin.

When my team went into the cabin for the first time, after the police had initially investigated it, it was in a state of disrepair. There were cups and plates with food covered in mold, and there was mold growing in the shower. The entire house smelled like copper. We initially believed that Emily Peter created this state of living for herself. If this was the permanent state of her cabin, then it would make sense why she would never want people to go there.

Not much can be said about Emily Peter's tendency to easily be distracted by things. Although we have not ruled out the possibility of an undiagnosed mental condition, I believe that this behavior seems more natural than concerning.

45

11-20-19

Not much has happened in the last few days. I called my mom. She still insists it is too dangerous for me to live out here with only a landline and a portable radio. I want the least amount of distractions as possible. I know that if I had an emergency, it would be harder for me to get help, but not much happens in this place. She's far more worried than she needs to be.

I wrote some today, but none of it was any good. I'm hoping that a drive to and walk along the Carriage Trail will help clear my mind so I can get some real writing done.

| Charles Investigative Company |
Charleston, West Virginia

Notes:

We have spoken on many occasions with Emily Peter's mother. She told us about their weekly calls and often expresses regret over not encouraging her daughter to prepare even more for an emergency.

I suspect that, if Emily Peter did have some sort of break in her mental well-being, it would have happened between this entry and the one after it because, as stated i n the following entry, this is the first day in which she mentions Jane Doles.

Despite whatever standing her mental health had been in, Emily Peter continued to call her mom on their regular schedule for two weeks. When we asked Peter's mother if she noticed any differences in her daughter's behavior or speech, she said that she did not. Once again, she expressed regret over not paying more attention to her daughter.

11-20-19

Evening

 I don't usually journal in the evenings, but I thought that I should make an exception.

 I met someone strange on the Carriage Trail today.

 I saw a woman dressed in a white gown that ended just below her knees. She was holding onto a knitted shawl that was wrapped across her shoulders. She clung to the shawl tightly, although she didn't seem to be cold. She wore brown boots and thick knitted socks that peaked out from her boots.

 I had planned to walk past her when she called out to me.

 "Excuse me, Miss," she said with a thick southern drawl. Almost no one in Charleston has a southern accent. Maybe she was from out of town.

 "Do you need help?" It was the first thing that I could think of to ask her. Someone who was dressed like that on the trail must have gotten lost or something. Or wandered away from home.

 She told me that she lived in the neighborhood at the top of the trail. She said that she regularly went on walks because she was prone to small fits of cabin fever.

 I asked her if she stayed in her house all

day when she wasn't walking.

She said yes.

I asked her why I hadn't seen her before, since I come to the trail everyday. She didn't answer. Instead, she asked me if I would walk with her. I said that I would, although, I am not quite sure why I did this.

I think that, in some ways, I felt bad for her. I'm not sure what for, though. Was it her clothes? Was it her desire to make a connection with another human being? She must be lonely. I think she wanted someone to talk to. If this is what people can define as a friend: someone to talk to, I guess I wanted to be her friend. I don't know why I wanted this, but I knew that I did.

I feel sick.

There were lots of people around so I didn't feel unsafe walking with her.

In the end, she just wanted someone to talk to. I told her my name, and she said that her name was Jane Doles. She asked me why I came to the Carriage Trail, and I thought that question was strange. Everyone comes to the trail to walk and admire the scenery.

I told her how I'm a writer, that walking here helps me to clear my head. She asked me what I wrote, and I said lots of things, but none of them had the meanings that I wanted to convey. She asked me what were the meanings I wanted to convey. I said something that will change some people for the good and others for the worst. She said that was probably too vague of an idea to work off of, and I told her that I knew.

And so we talked like this for a while. She mostly asked the questions, and I mostly gave the answers. I didn't really know what questions to ask her. I made a pathetic attempt of asking if she knew of any new shops and restaurants I should visit. Instead of answering, she asked if I was new to the area, and then we went into a long conversation about how often I visited in West Virginia and what it was like to live in Pittsburgh.

We didn't stop talking until we reached the bottom of the trail again (this was our fourth or fifth time we walked up and down the trail). I said that I should probably get back. The sun was beginning to set - it always sets so early at the end of November - and I don't really like driving in the dark. She told me goodbye. I asked her if she felt safe going to her home by herself.

I might watch too much true crime stuff.

She said that she was okay and so we said goodbye to each other.

As I was driving home, and even when I reached the cabin, I couldn't stop thinking about her eyes. She hardly took her gaze away from staring at the ground. When she did, she would look at me. Her eyes were a light shade of gray. Her pupils should have been black, but they were just a slightly darker shade of gray. When she stared at me, I was the one looking at the ground.

| Charles Investigative Company |
Charleston, West Virginia

Notes:

There is no known person who goes by the name of Jane Doles who matches this appearance, and lives in the place that Emily Peter was staying at the time of her disappearance. It is possible, however, that Jane Doles is a false name or alias, and the person who uses this name is involved in the case. We have found a few people that are close resemblance to the description that Emily Peter provides, but so far, none with the distinct gray eyes that Emily Peter mentions.

We have spoken with a few people who regularly saw Emily Peter walking along the Carriage Trail. Some have s aid that occasionally they observed Emily Peter talking to herself while walking. This is not necessarily unusual behavior, however, when we asked these individuals to detail further about Emily Peter's behavior, they said that, often, there would be long pauses during talks. She would also occasionally look to her side while she was talking, as if to someone else entirely.

It is in my opinion that Emily Peters created Jane Doles in her mind as a way to help work through her lack of inspiration or any other stressors she had been experiencing. If Emily Peter did suffer some sort of mental break, it is likely that it happened during this walk.

11-30-19

 I spend more time at the Carriage Trail now. It used to be my habit to write in the morning. Now, I sleep through the mornings and spend entire afternoons and evenings walking the trail. When I return home, I write through the night. I have had bursts of productivity before in my career, but never so much as this. I am writing more than I've ever done before.

 It is Jane who is inspiring me. I don't see her everyday, but I always stay until the sun is about to set to see if she will arrive. I am not obsessed with her as a person, but I think that I might be obsessed with the inspiration I have after I see her. I have the worst time writing when I don't see her.

 On the occasions that I do see her, she is always wearing the same exact outfit she wore when I first met her. I asked her about this, seeing as how it is only becoming colder every day and her nightgown, shawl, socks, and boots don't seem to keep her warm. She always tells me that they are good enough. Then she changes the topic.

 I wonder what her home life is like. I haven't asked her about it though. It seems too personal. She's always quick to dismiss personal questions.

 She talks about her family occasionally, though,

in bits and pieces. She told me that she liked to cook with her mother. That was the best memory she had of her - them cooking together on a winter evening while the heat from the stove made the whole house warm. She said that her dad was always working. And when he wasn't, he didn't pay much attention to her. She didn't have a lot of memories of him. I asked her who he paid attention to instead. It was one of the only personal questions I have asked her that she has answered.

"My brother," she said simply.

I asked her what her brother was like. Since she spoke of her parents in the past tense, I assumed that they had passed away. Her brother might be the only close family she has left.

All she told me was, "It's complicated."

An unusual answer, but I didn't ask her further.

Most of our conversations are about my writing. I have been able to outline all of my current work just with the conversations I have had with her. Even though I usually feel nervous when I talk through my story ideas with people, I don't with her.

I don't have to worry about saying the wrong thing when I'm with Jane. She's calm, and if she doesn't like what I say, she just dismisses it instead of getting angry.

When Jane sees that I have come to join her on the trail she always smiles. It is a closed-lipped smile, but it is the only time I ever see her smile. She looks so sad most of the time. If I can make her happy, make her day better, even if just a little bit...

| Charles Investigative Company |
Charleston, West Virginia

Notes:

Operating under the assumption that Doles is indeed a real person, all of Emily Peter's notes imply that Doles was hiding something. Doles's strong desire to want to know everything about Peter while revealing very little about herself is especially concerning. This pattern leads me to believe that Emily Peter could have potentially fallen into a trap that Jane Doles had set up through a false friendship built up before Peter went missing. I am sorry that I cannot provide another phrase other than this metaphor. "Falling into a trap" is the best that I can say with so few leads in this case.

If, however, Jane Doles is a manifestation created by Emily Peter, then the lack of information Jane Doles gave about herself could make her seem real. The less Emily Peter had to think about Jane Doles's backstory, the more she could focus on an image of them walking with her.

We can confirm that Emily Peter was going through a stage of productivity in her writing career during this time. When Emily Peter was reported missing and we were assigned to this case, my team collected all of the writings we were able to retrieve from the local police and from the cabin she stayed in. These writings continue to be extremely helpful because she dated all of her writings on the days she wrote them.

I assume that this was her way to track her progress.

Emily Peter worked on several stories during this time – a collection of shorter pieces and novels – all of them seem to be unfinished. The longest piece she had been working on is a novel titled *Danse Macabre*. The novel is about 100 pages long, and it is in our files. What follows is a brief description of the novel:

The main character in the novel is Alice, who, for most of the novel, is walking on a trail. On this trail, she meets several different creatures that masquerade as humans. With a few given flashbacks, we come to learn that each of these creatures represented one of Alice's bad habits, which are also referred to in the novel as Alice's inner demons. Halfway through the novel, Alice figures out that she is not actually walking by her own desire. Instead, the creatures are controlling her movements. The novel does not have an official ending, but where Emily Peter left off, Alice was walking deeper into the forest. She had suffered several wounds and a broken ankle from different incidents, but the creatures would not let her stop moving.

The novel has a dark tone. It is not definite proof of Emily Peter's mental instability, but after reading it and coming to the more informal, slightly light-hearted tone of this journal, it was enough to make me feel unsettled whenever I think of the different mindsets Emily Peter was in during this time.

12-1-19

I haven't slept much. I went to bed about 4 or 5 am last night. Or, rather this morning. I don't really keep track of the hours when I am writing and when I go asleep, but I am pretty sure I went to sleep around that time.

I woke up at 6:30am by a loud banging coming from near my house. I know this time for certain, though, because I checked the clock when I woke up.

I laid in bed for a while. I thought that someone had broken in, and if I had moved, they would be able to hear me and know where I was. Except, I did move, very slightly, to grab the knife I keep in the top cabinet of my nightstand. I know a lot of people around me have guns. I don't like guns, and so I don't own any. I do keep a knife in my nightstand and a baseball bat beside my closed bedroom door, just in case.

I heard the noise again and again, and then a pause. It was like someone was using all of the force within their body to slam against my garage door. A loud bang and then a rattling sound.

I kept one hand on my knife, and the other on my mouth. I wanted to cry, but tears wouldn't come.

The sound came in threes and then a pause. It

was so loud. I swear that, when the sound came, the walls of my cabin would shake, but it was too dark in my room to tell.

I thought that, for a sound to be that loud, it would have to come from directly outside of or inside of my house, but it wasn't. It did not grow louder. It did not grow closer. The sound, unbelievably loud, remained the same. It was coming from further away from the cabin.

I crept over to the window. The knife was still in my hand, and I had grabbed the baseball bat when I had gotten up.

I had half-hoped, half-believed that maybe it was some type of construction work happening down the street. I peeked out from the curtain, and the street was bare.

The sound came again, in threes, and I opened the curtains slightly wider and looked around. There was still nothing. I was about to abandon my efforts in the hopes that I would be able to get downstairs fast enough to go to the phone and call 911, when I saw, in the woods near the back of my cabin, a tall shadow swaying in a near-by tree. It looked like the outline of a man, except; everything was much longer than it needed to be. Its arms reached to the ground, where its hands curled when they met the ground. When it swayed, its knees bent in crooked arcs and its head bobbed up and down. When I saw it, the sound stopped. It was on its second noise and had not completed its third yet, but it had stopped.

I ended up calling 911, and they sent the police. While they were on their way, I went back up to my bedroom and locked the door. I peeked out of the curtains once more, but I could no longer see the figure. Sure it had moved and was makings its way closer, I stayed in the corner of my room. I tried to muffle my own cries. I waited for the banging sound to start again. It never did.

When the police arrived, they found nothing. They asked me what the figure looked like, and when I told them, they asked me when I had seen it. They implied that I had dreamt the whole thing.

I was awake. It couldn't have been a dream.

They left after that, and I haven't left my bedroom for most of the day. I've barely eaten, and I don't dare go back to sleep.

I am afraid to leave, but I need to go to the Carriage Trail.

| Charles Investigative Company |
Charleston, West Virginia

Notes:

This journal entry is one of the more baffling parts of the case. Since shadows often appear longer than a person, it is very possible that there was someone in the woods, watching Emily Peter's cabin, and she only saw the shadow of this person. The distorted image of the shadow that Emily Peter provides could also be an illusion created by whatever instrument the person was holding onto to make the sounds that Peter describes hearing.

None of Peter's neighbors heard the noise she claims to have heard. However, when we asked them if they heard anything unusual on the date that Emily Peter provided, almost all of them asked if we could be more specific. We gave them more specific details using descriptions from Emily Peter's writing. All of them said that they had not seen or heard anything similar to what Emily Peter described having seen or heard. However, there was one man who grew up in the particular part of West Virginia. He said that he had not seen or heard anything unusual that night, but our descriptions reminded him of The Silencer. We asked him if he could elaborate on this, and what follows is a summary of what he told us:

The Legend of the Silencer regards a creature that lives in the forests outside of Charleston, West Virginia. The creature is described as being tall, lanky, with limbs that bend at odd angles. Every part of it sways when it moves because it is not strong enough to keep itself upright. It can also bend quite easily, since it has very few muscles and bones. It often climbs trees in the nearby forests in West Virginia, and it bends across the branches. It screams, and if you are close enough to it, its screams will burst your eardrums. Once you are taken over from the pain, it will crawl on top of you so that its entire body is bent and wraps around you. It then crushes all of your bones and eats you alive.

We asked him if this legend was based on any true events. He said that it was just a story that parents told their children to keep them from wandering off too deep into the woods so they would not get lost. We asked him if there had been any strange events in this area that had any correlation to this legend. He told us that, if there were any, he could not remember them, and he was likely to remember something like that. There is a recorded version of our conversation on file.

We have analyzed several newspaper documents and journals pertaining to this area from the West Virginia Archives, and we can confirm that there are no recorded events that bear any correlation to this legend.

Emily Peter mentioned that she kept a knife by her nightstand. We can neither confirm nor deny this because, when we went thro ugh Emily Peter's cabin, we found no knives. Every single knife in the cabin was gone. This is a small detail to note, but I thought that it should be noted, nonetheless.

12-1-19

I am sure that I am being followed now by the same creature. I saw it again at the Carriage Trail.

Jane was at the Carriage Trail today. I told her everything that happened. She said that I shouldn't have come to the trail, I should have stayed home and slept instead.

"It is dangerous to drive without sleep," she told me.

I knew, but I needed to talk with someone to make sure I wasn't going crazy. She said that I wasn't, but beyond that, she didn't say anything else.

Jane and I never walk past the monument towards the front of the trail, the one that was made for the two women who were killed and buried on the trail.

The first time I had started talking to her, we reached the monument, and she told me that we should turn around and walk again. We followed this routine for all of our other conversations, and I never questioned it.

Today, we just walked in silence. I walked past the monument. I didn't notice until I looked up and saw a shadow in the corner of my vision. I thought it was Jane, but it was too far away to be Jane. I turned to it - I really wasn't thinking - but I turned to it, and there, standing between the trees, was the shadow. Its arms were wrapped around a branch, and it was swaying. It opened its mouth, and I ran.

I could only think about getting to my car. It wasn't until my keys dropped from my shaking hands into a puddle that I realized I had forgotten about Jane. I am so sorry, Jane.

I looked around to see if the creature was there, but I saw nothing. Not a single person either. Had Jane and I been the only ones on the trail the entire time? No, that couldn't have been right. I remember passing people on the trail, but there were no cars in the parking lot, and there were no shadows moving in the forest.

I only stared at the trail as I ran back to Jane.

What if it had gotten to her?

She was still standing past the monument.

"Oh Jane, thank God—"

"Where did you go?" Her voice was strained and tears filmed over her gray eyes.

"Jane, it was there. The thing I saw this morning. I tried to run away; why didn't you?"

"Emily, there was no creature."

And I just stood there. I felt the back of my throat tighten. How could she have not seen it?

"You're sleep deprived. You need to go back home and get some sleep."

"Can I stay at your house tonight?" My voice broke apart, and I felt a tear slide down my face. I wiped it away.

"No. I think that it's better if you stay at your place tonight. The sun is about to set. You need to go home."

"Will you be back here tomorrow?"

"Only if you get enough sleep," she said and started walking up the hill again to wherever her house was.

I walked back to my car. I drove a lot faster than I should have. I didn't realize I was driving so fast until the end of the ride, when I looked down and saw the speed.

I didn't look out to the forest as I walked up the steps to the cabin. Once inside, I checked all of the doors and windows. None of them had been broken or unlocked.

I took the sleeping pills a few minutes ago. I locked my bedroom door, so, if someone does break in, I will be able to hear it.

| Charles Investigative Company |
Charleston, West Virginia

Notes:

I will start off this note with aspects about this journal entry that we know are true:

- Emily Peter did take sleeping pills regularly.
- Specifically, she was prescribed Clonazepam, also known as Klonopin, but we also found Benadryl and Melatonin in her cabin. Her psychiatrist prescribed her sleeping pills after she lost her job working at a media production company in 2009. As indicated by her medical history, she has tried several different sleeping pills since 2009, but she has been taking Clonazepam for the past three years.
- Although Emily Peter eventually was able to live off of the money she earned from her writing, she never seemed to learn how to manage her stress over financial matters so as to prevent insomnia.
- She visited a few therapists over the years, but she never seemed to stay with any of them for longer than three appointments. All of this we know from contacting Emily Peter's doctor, whose statements are on file. We have not been able to contact any of the therapists who attempted to treat Emily Peter, but we hope that our efforts will be more successful in the immediate future.
- While the Carriage Trail is a popular place in Charleston, West Virginia, it sometimes does have few to no visitors.

- Peter mentioning that she noticed no one was at the Carriage Trail does not suggest a strange or unusual circumstance that prompts more attention to be dedicated to this part of the entry.

What strikes me as strange about this entry is Jane Doles' response to the creature Emily Peter describes. Previous reports mention that the creature was a result of Emily Peter's sleep deprivation and her manifestation of Jane Doles was her rational mind trying to make sense to her that the creature was a figment of her sleep deprivation.

I find that unlikely however, as in most cases, a person needs to go without sleep for much longer than a single night to begin hallucinating. It is also entirely possible that Emily came across the "Legend of the Silencer" during her research for her stories, though we did not find any indication of such, it could have left a large enough impression on her to make her believe that she saw the creature in her sleep-deprived state. However, this is only speculation.As we have not been able to disprove the existence of Jane Doles, we still have not eliminated the possibility that Jane Doles is out there somewhere. If she is, this journal entry is peculiar because of her response and behavior in this particular situation. Her unwillingness to walk past this monument, which is when Emily Peter saw the creature, suggests (although I must say that this suggestion is not based in any sort of reliable evidence) that Jane Doles was working with a partner. In this situation, Jane Doles and her partner were attempting to confuse and scare Emily until she reached a breaking point.

| Charles Investigative Company |
Charleston, West Virginia

Notes:

The kidnapping and/or murder of Emily Peter is an ongoing possibility of this case. However, it is not a leading aspect of this case because of the following:

1.We have found no suspects that match the description of Jane Doles

2.The Peter family does not have any known enemies

3.Emily Peter's body has not been found, and there have been no reported sightings of anyone seeing her in the surrounding states.

With this being said, if Emily Peter was kidnapped, it was likely by Jane Doles and another possible unknown partner.

Side note: Emily Peter was not known to have suffered from any forms of any hallucinations, including seeing what are commonly referred to as "shadow people" in sleep paralysis. This is the main reason as to why I, personally, doubt that Emily Peter entirely imagined the creature she saw in the woods.

12-3-19

I called Mom today. I didn't tell her about what happened. We had our normal conversation. I responded as usual, although her efforts to convince me that I should take emergency situations more seriously were harder to deny this time. I didn't tell her this, though, because then she would have asked me why I changed my mind. I would have had to tell her. I don't know how I could have held it back, so I just continued with the conversation as we usually had it. If I had told her what happened, she would have wanted me to go home and stay there for a while until we figured all of this out. She couldn't have forced me to go home, but she would have put up a damn good effort. I'm not sure why, but the thought of leaving here makes me want to throw up.

I am not going to the Carriage Trail today. It's raining outside. That doesn't usually stop me. But right now the thought of walking outside, even with a raincoat on and an umbrella, makes me feel empty inside. I know that's a stupid way to describe this feeling, but I don't really want to write more about it.

This will be the first day that I don't write, and maybe that will be a good thing. It's good to take a break from things every once in a while.

Jane will understand why I'm not at the trail today. She doesn't show up when it's raining anyway.

| Charles Investigative Company |
Charleston, West Virginia

Notes:

Emily Peter did not want to leave West Virginia. Or did she just not want to go home? Could that have been reason enough to cause her to hide away?

Although it is nearly impossible to search an entire state, especially one that has such remote regions as West Virginia has, we have made extensive efforts to search as much of the state as possible. Though we have not found any evidence of Emily Peter's whereabouts, it does not entirely eliminate the possibility that she is still in the state. We have conducted parallel investigations and searches in Ohio, Kentucky, Virginia, Pennsylvania, Maryland, and Delaware on the basis that Emily could be in of these States. The details of these searches and investigations are in our files on this case, and the searches in Virginia and Kentucky are ongoing.

Emily Peter's mother does recall ha ving this phone call with her daughter. She does not remember if there was anything unusual about their conversation. She does recall that it was difficult to hear her daughter because her voice would fade in and out, like she was driving through a tunnel while she was calling her. The mother does confirm that she brought up this concern to her daughter multiple times during their call. Emily Peter's only known phone that she used while she was at the cabin was a landline (side note: the landline was one that was attached to the wall and connected by a cord), she would not have been able to bring the phone into her car and call someone from it.

Her mother was also concerned about Emily staying in West Virginia through December, since she always left West Virginia at the end of November. However, when she brought up this concern, her daughter did not respond. Eventually, the mother changed the topic.

12-3-19

I keep hearing the creature. It is too far away to see it. Too far for it to shake the walls of the cabin like it did the first time. It won't go away. Bang, bang, bang, quiet. Bang, bang, bang, quiet. Over and over again. It is in the back of my head. I cannot get rid of it. I know what it sounds like now. I have heard it so much that I can finally tell what the sound is. Balloons popping. One by one they go. Bang, bang, bang, pop, pop, pop. It's the same sound. When it gets louder, it sounds like a thousand balloons popping all at once. Each of the sounds blends into the other, and then quiet.

And then it starts again.

I am going to the Carriage Trail. I need to clear my head. I don't know if Jane will be there. Tonight, I don't really care. I need to walk around someplace else to stop hearing those sounds.

Notes:

I cannot say what mental state Emily Peter was in at the time of writing this. She is showing different traits from various mental conditions, including aspects of high functioning anxiety and paranoia.

However, if Emily Peter was kidnapped , these sounds could have been created by an outside source – such as Jane Doles' accomplice – to send Emily Peter to a breaking point.

This journal entry concerns me for many reasons, but the journal entry that follows it concerns me even more. Thus, I will leave my conclusions to the analysis of that entry.

Evening

I don't know where to start with this. I know that I must write down what happened because it is important, but I don't know where to start.

I went to the Carriage Trail. I will start there.

I went to the trail. Jane was there. She looked concerned when she saw me.

I can't believe that I'm remembering that little detail right now, but she did. As soon as she saw me, she frowned and her eyes crinkled at the edges.

"You look worse," she said.

"Yeah," was my response. The conversation ended right then and there.

I don't know how long we walked. The crunch of our footsteps against the pebbles and gravel on the trail was enough to clear my head eventually.

I'm not sure if anything happened between that point where everything was quiet and then when the sound returned.

It was behind us. It was so loud. Too loud. It brought bursts of black dots across my vision. Bang, bang, bang, pop, pop, pop—quiet. Tears burned into my eyes. Why? Why was it back? How had it found me? I saw Jane, and her eyes were just as large as mine.

"Can you hear that?" I yelled at her over the sound.

She nodded and put one finger to her lips. She took my hand, and we ran into the forest. We shouldn't have done that. All of the trees were bare, nothing but sticks to hide behind.

We should have run to my car.

The sound came in threes again.

I leaned in as close to Jane as I could.

"What is that?"

She had covered her face with her hands and her shoulders were heaving. When she dropped her hands into her lap, her face was crinkled, as if she had been crying. There were no tears in her eyes or on her face.

She leaned in close to me. "He always comes for me," she said. "He's stuck, and he doesn't realize that he can stop. He always comes for me. It wasn't even me. It was my brother. Why can't he understand that?"

"Who comes for you? Jane?"

"I should have never talked to you, but I am so lonely. He's come for you too. They always die. Every single one of them, and when you die, you won't be the same."

"Jane, what do you –"

It was very subtle, but it was there. Footsteps crunching on the gravel.

I covered Jane's mouth, but he appeared behind her as soon as my hand reached up to her face.

"I am so sorry, Emily."

I heard the voice before I saw him.

"You think you can keep secrets from us?" He asked.

I tried to grab Jane's hand. I swear that I was holding onto it. I swear she was running with me the entire time down the hill and when we made it to the car, I really thought we had gotten away.

It wasn't until I pulled my keys out of my pocket that I realized my other hand was empty.

That was when I heard the gun go off three times.

From that distance, it sounded like a thousand balloons popping in successive order. That's probably a stupid way to describe it, but that's the only thing I can think of right now.

I drove to the police station. It's a miracle I didn't crash. I wasn't in any state to drive.

Somebody at the station helped me to calm down when I got there. The people couldn't take a statement from me until I was able to form words. They went through some breathing exercises with me that really helped. And then I told them everything that had happened.

I don't really want to write about it - the trail, the police station - anymore."

I am back at home now, which is why I am writing this. The police officers gave me another phone that I was only to use for the near future until we know that whoever shot Jane is not after me as well.

I took sleeping pills again.

I am so sorry, Jane. I wish that I could have saved you.

| Charles Investigative Company |
Charleston, West Virginia

Notes:

This is the last journal entry Emily Peter made before she went missing. She was reported to be missing by a police officer who was meant to check on her the morning after her final entry. When she did not respond to the phone call and the officer did not hear a response from her after knocking on her door, a few of the officers went to her house. She was not in the cabin.

As of May 12, 2021, she is still missing.

The first thing my team did was try to identify the shooter that Emily mentions in the final entry. We have had many suspects, but none of them have proven to be the armed man.

Emily Peter did not describe the man in great detail, it is much harder to find suspects. She did, however, describe the armed man at the police station. We have a typed version of the recorded interview that Emily Peter gave at the police station on our files, but I will write a summary of Emily Peter's description of the man below:

He wore long, green, baggy pants and a white, loose shirt. She thought it was a long-sleeve shirt. He wore a hat, although she did not look up at his face long enough to tell what kind of hat it was; she could just see it in the corner of her vision. He was Caucasian, and he had a thick, Southern accent. She did not know what type of gun he had, but she saw that it was long and narrow. Almost as long as his arm. She was asked if she could give any more details about his appearance – if he had any noticeable scars or tattoos – or if she saw any more of his face. She said that she really had not been able to see his face, and if he had tattoos or scars, they were covered by his clothing. A small but noted detail that Emily Peter said was, "he really wasn't dressed for winter."

This description gave us a starting point to look for the man based on his location and clothing. We began our investigation by talking with the people who live near the Carriage Trail in Charleston. All of our discussions with these people are in our files. As stated before, we still have not found the armed man or Jane Doles.

Further Notes:

We have reason to suspect that, if Jane Doles kidnapped Emily Peter, the armed man was her accomplice. Since Emily Peter did not see the man shoot Jane Doles, nor did Jane Doles run after Emily Peter, it is a possibility that the event was staged. If this was the case, we do not understand why Jane Doles would have wanted Emily to inform the police, but our lack of understanding does not rule thi s out as a possibility.

Of course, we cannot rule out the mental state of Emily Peter at the time. We do not have enough evidence to prove or deny that she had suffered any sort of mental instability, but until we find Emily Peter, this cannot be ruled out as a possibility.

While analyzing Emily Peter's journal entries did not provide me with more evidence, as I hoped it would, my team and I will not stop our efforts in looking for Emily Peter. My only wish is that my team and I will be able to find Emily Peter so that we may bring solace to her family.

DON'T GO INTO THE LAKE

"Do you think there'll still be enough light for us to finish our drawings?" Mia asked in her childlike voice that always seemed to calm rather than annoy. It was just past five. The sky still held the afternoon sun, but it would be dark before too long.

"Yeah, we'll have plenty of time. As long as we get the outlines of the Ferris wheel and buses and swings, we should be good. We can always add in our interpretations of the colors later. Isn't that what Mrs. Bucker is always talking about, adding in our own touches and stuff?" Jack replied.

Mia slumped back further into her car seat. "Sort of," she said.

I've seen Mia spend entire months on one drawing when the rest of the class had already completed several. If it wasn't exact, it wasn't good enough for her. The thought of not getting the colors right on the dot would make her hate her pictures, even if they looked perfect.

"We can always come back, you know," I said. "If we wanted to finish our drawings."

"That, we can do," Jack agreed. He had one hand on the steering wheel and the other on the dashboard, where he tapped out the tune on the radio. I grabbed onto the edge of the seat as the car tipped to the right and then to the left.

When the trees ended along the road, I saw the buses. They were stripped to expose their gray metal with dark spots, most likely water stains from spending years stuck in summer rainstorms.

I breathed in and out and coughed at the intake of dust. There was a hollow feeling in my chest. The cloth on the car seat was digging into my skin more than it had the whole ride. Even though the air conditioning was blasting, heat rose into my face.

I thought that maybe I should stay in the car and take a nap. The others could wake me when they're finished.

From the corner of my eye, I watched Mia bring her pink case of art supplies closer to her chest, her knuckles turning white.

The car rumbled until Jack brought it to a complete stop. He rolled down his window and screamed a big, loud, satisfied scream. The sound made me jump, and I clung to my chest to calm my racing heart. I could feel the blood pounding into the edges of my head.

"This is incredible!" He yelled while turning back to face us. "Imagine what it will look like against the sunset!"

I opened my mouth to disagree, but Mia beat me to it.

"We're not staying until sunset."

"Come on! We need to see what it looks like. We could make a theme out of it. You know, how the beauty of nature overtakes man's worst creations or something like that."

A laugh rose into the back of my throat. I bit down on my lip to keep it from spilling out. Jack could take criticism, but he was always embarrassed whenever people laughed at him.

"Okay, just the sunset, and then we're leaving," Mia said. Jack reached over and gave Mia a high-five. She raised her hand just in time for him to miss her face.

"You won't regret this. It's going to be so beautiful. I just know it. I can feel it."

"I better not," Mia said and opened her car door. Jack and I opened ours and got out as well.

It was muggy outside, and the hot air clung to my skin. I held my left hand across my forehead to shield my vision from the sun. In the distance ahead of me was the Ferris wheel. Its copper-colored chairs swung lazily in the breeze. Green and yellowing leaves decorated the vines that gripped the steel structure. Bushes and overgrowth formed the structure's base, and the lake was beside it

"I guess you want the Ferris wheel?" I asked Jack.

"Yeah, I mean, if you guys don't mind."

Both Mia and I shook our heads.

"I wanted the buses anyway," Mia said. "It'll be quicker for me to draw those and get all of the colors finished in time. I think there was some stuff in the buses too that I want to try and draw."

"I'll take the swings then," I said. "My brother told me there's some stuffed animals and toys on them. I'm going to try to draw close-ups of those first, and then the swings."

Jack clapped his hands together. "We are so going to get a hundred on this project."

"Enough to bring up your grade?" I teased.

"Let's hope so."

Mia gave a short laugh before covering her mouth with her hand. I smiled too. Jack started walking toward the Ferris wheel, and Mia waved goodbye to me before she walked to the buses.

The swings created lazy moans on their rusty hinges. The wind carried their uneven tune past the red letters against the black sign that spelled out "Lake Shawnee" as I walked past it.

Some of the swings' seats had rusted to the point that they could no longer hold onto their chains. Instead, they dangled from only one or rested on the ground, where vines grew over them.

A teddy bear – about the size of my hand – smiled back at me from one of the seats. His once white fur was clumped together and patched with filth.

It wasn't alive. It couldn't understand what it was like to be out here, but the bear struck a chord within me. I wanted to take it back home, but this place was abandoned. *Let it be abandoned,* I reminded myself.

I sat down on the grass and placed my sketchbook across my lap. I started sketching a close-up of the teddy bear first. Its little fuzzy ears; its black beady eyes...

The wind picked up, and chills ran from my shoulders and down my arms. I felt a tickle at the corner of my ear.

"Don't go into the lake," a high-pitched, gentle voice said.

"Mia, how did you..." I turned to the side, but no one was there. My pencil fell through my fingertips. Jack was sitting by the

Ferris wheel. I couldn't see Mia. She had to be by the buses. I would've heard her walk over here, but I still got up to check.

Jack didn't even notice when I started walking toward him. He was crouched over his drawing, obscuring the view of anything he had already completed, but Mia heard my footsteps. She lifted her head and asked, "Hey, what's up?"

"Oh, nothing," I fumbled and let out a sigh. "I was just stretching my legs."

She nodded and said, "Check out my drawing." She held the picture up to me, and at first, I didn't quite understand what I was looking at. Wasn't Mia supposed to be sketching the buses? On the paper, there was a single circle, outlined in black, with green half-circles on it. The half-circles were colored in, and in the middle of the circle, were two stick figures holding hands.

I gave a short laugh, and then asked, "What is it supposed to be?"

Mia rolled her eyes at me. "The buses, silly."

I couldn't tell if she was joking, so I asked, "Is it something in the buses?"

Mia shrugged. "Maybe."

I leaned back and stared at Mia, but she turned away from me and went back to sketching.

"Mia, are you okay?"

"Yes," she said. "Now get back to sketching, or we won't get it finished today."

I stayed there for a moment more. But, when Mia didn't acknowledge me after a couple of minutes, I started to walk away. *Maybe being weird is a part of her creative process.*

The lake was behind the Ferris wheel. I didn't go any closer to it than I already was, but I could see it had murky waters.

It had probably come from a child playing in the hills nearby and screamed out the warning. *The wind could've carried her voice,* I tried to convince myself as I sat back down on the same patch of grass.

As I began to sketch again, each line I drew made my mind rest a little easier.

~

The cold brought goose bumps to my skin. I placed my pencil on my sketchbook while I wrapped my arms around my chest. As I looked around, I saw that the clouds were brushed in soft pinks against golden and violet lines.

I cupped my hands around my mouth and yelled, "Jack, the sunset!"

He was still crouched over his drawing but turned to look at me.

"Oh my God," he stammered. His sketchbook and art supplies rolled off his lap and onto the ground as he stood up. He raked his fingers through his hair and howled at the sky around him. I could hear Mia laughing as I walked toward them, and I couldn't help but join in the laughter.

"I mean, just look at this! Look at the Ferris wheel!" He started running forward. "Look at the lake!"

As I watched him, a brush of cold air ran across my neck and shoulders. Burning nausea settled into the bottom of my stomach. Behind him, on the other side of the lake, there was a little girl. But was she little? She was as tall as Mia and had her same blonde – almost white – hair.

"Don't go near the lake," I mumbled, but no one heard me. He was only a foot away from the lake and walking ever closer to it.

"Look at how the light reflects off of here!" He said.

"Don't!" The scream rose in the back of my throat. "Don't go near the lake!"

Jack turned to me.

As he did so, I watched as his foot stumbled at the lake's edge. He reached out, but he only grabbed onto the air. He crashed into the lake, and droplets splattered onto the edge.

The girl stood where Jack once was, and for a moment, I thought Mia had somehow reached him before I did. I stopped.

"Come on," Mia yelled. I turned to look at her, and when I looked back, the girl was gone.

As I got closer, I only saw Jack's hands struggling over the water's surface. Bubbles formed around him.

Mia was there before I was. She laid on the edge and held onto a root poking out of the ground. With her other hand, she reached out to Jack. His hands wavered, coming out of the water and going back down in rhythm.

I lay beside Mia and reached out for his other hand.

Mia leaned forward ever so slightly. She grimaced. I had enough time to see her red face before Jack grabbed my hand. I stared at the hand around mine, not fully realizing what he had just done. When his hand started to drag me into the lake with him, I broke out of my trance. I dug my knees into the ground and started pulling.

It was muddy, and I slid forward. I held onto his hand with both of mine, and I wouldn't let go, even as my stomach ached from trying to pull back, and sweat trickled down my brow and into my eyes.

In the corner of my vision, I watched as Mia fell forward. I couldn't turn to look at her, though, because at that moment, Jack's head appeared above the water.

He started coughing and muttering something. Something that was lost to the wind until I could make it out.

"I'm stuck," he mumbled, and even though I could make this out, I continued to pull.

Jack screamed. Like nails on a chalkboard.

I pushed harder into the ground. Jack's arm reached the surface and then his chest. Mia and I gave one last pull, and his stomach touched the ground. As I let go of my grasp and Jack's hand slipped through mine, I fell back. Black spots danced at the edges of my vision, covering the flames in the sky.

I rolled over onto my side and curled up. I closed my eyes. My whole body was shaking, and I felt like I couldn't get enough breaths in me.

And then a scream, sharp enough to break glass, pierced through me.

I opened my eyes faster than I should have. At first, I was only able to see shadows. I blinked them back and saw the outline of someone crouching over a body on the ground. Then, I realized it was Mia huddled over Jack.

Except, she stood over his legs. I thought that was odd.

I tried to stand up but was met with a wave of dizziness. Mia screamed again as I tried to regain my footing.

One step forward, and I stumbled two steps back.

"Help me!" Mia yelled.

The vision of her was pulsating around me, and I saw nothing but red around Jack's ankles. Mia moved to Jack's torso and tried to put her hands under his armpits.

"Don't just stand there!" Mia grumbled, and as I blinked a few more times, my vision settled. I found that I was first able to walk to her, and after gaining my footing, I began running.

My vision remained constant, but I almost wished the darkness would've returned when I saw Jack's foot.

His ankle was turned upwards so that the front was almost touching his leg. His bone, broken and jagged, protruded from his skin.

Mia let go of one side of his armpit, and I grabbed onto the other one. In order to do so, I had to look past Mia's shoulders while she moved to Jack's left side.

There was the girl again. She was leaning down, her hand reaching out to the water.

Mia started to drag Jack forward, and the movement was enough for me to turn back and focus on him. He screamed until his voice broke apart. The bone in his ankle was dragging a line in the ground with him.

"Can you hold onto him on this side?" I heard Mia ask, but the question didn't register at first. I felt like I was going to throw up.

"There are things down there. So deep," Jack was rambling. His words turned into slurring as Mia laid him back down.

"Can you grab his other shoulder?"

"I-I think so," I said.

Mia nodded and moved to his leg. "We have to try not to make it any worse," I heard her mutter.

"Mia...Mia," Jack said.

Mia lifted his leg, and Jack started screaming again. The sound made her jump and drop his leg back down.

Jack was tall – over six feet – and at his shoulders, we had seemed so far away from the lake. But, when Mia jumped, she was at the edge where his leg was. She couldn't grab onto anything as she fell back.

When the girl was beside her, I realized they were not the same: the same hair, almost the same height, but her skin, I don't know how I didn't notice this earlier, but it was clear to me when she stood next to Mia.

Her skin was gray and puffed up like a balloon. Black, beetle-like insects crawled down her arms. When she grabbed onto Mia, brown, green liquid spewed around them, staining Mia's clothes.

Mia screamed as the thing tried to pull her down. She clawed at its arms, breaking its skin, which folded over its arms and exposed black muscles that beat in tune with its heart. A rancid oil smell filled the air.

The thing mimicked Mia's movement, dragging its nails across Mia's skin.

The air stood still around me, and pinpricks crawled up my arms. It felt like I had jumped into the freezing lake as I watched the lake water spill from Mia's skin.

This isn't right, I thought. *Where is the blood?*

Mia's screams echoed, filling my brain until I clawed at my head, feeling warm blood slide underneath my fingernails.

The creature lifted its hands, and I believed it was covering Mia's mouth. But, when its fingers reached the corners of her lips, it pulled.

As her skin broke apart, I saw Mia's blue eyes once more before a shadow passed over them. Her skin clung limply to her body, and underneath, green boils oozed against the black liquid where her muscles should have been.

The creature fell back, taking Mia with her into the lake.

"Why were you down there, Mia?" Jack mumbled. "Mia, why were you down there?"

THE SONG OF
BLENNERHASSETT ISLAND

The waves lapped over one another, drowning in the opaque waters below. Her song echoed across them. A soft, choking sound that could easily be heard as humming. It ran across my skin and brought chills down my arms. She stood at the edge of the island. Her gray dress whipped across her legs by the winds in the dark blue sky. She curled her arms and held them in front of her like she was meant to be holding something. She swung them back and forth at jagged angles while she continued to wail, and the waves carried her song.

In the hotel, the woman's cries still hummed in the back of my mind. I pressed the back of my hand to my forehead. It was a useless effort, and I did it more out of habit than anything. My hand was as warm as my forehead, and my fingers were trembling. As I stumbled down the hallway, I dragged one hand across the wall, steadying myself. Shadows danced at the edges of my vision, and along with them, children. Their laughter echoed, and lights flickered.

The numbers on the doors stood out in blurry spots; I could just make out three. Were we already on the third floor? The children were only steps away from me now, and they ran after one another like they were playing tag.

The girl had curly blond hair that clung close to her face. The boy's untied shoelaces clinked against the ground. He never stopped to tie them.

"You shouldn't be running," I tried to say, but what came out of my mouth was nothing more than a faint murmur. They ran down the stairs. Their footsteps clattered so that they echoed against the walls.

I clung to the railing. My feet skidded across the stairs. I felt myself falling forward despite being firmly on the ground. My heartbeat pounded into my fingertips.

I could still hear their laughter. When I turned past the door, they were still running only inches in front of me. I tried to steady myself, but I wasn't getting enough air. I heard music, muffled like it was coming from underneath the floorboards. A dull ringing persisted in the backs of my ears.

The children turned another corner in the hallway, and sharp pinpricks ran through my back and down my arms. Hundreds of people were beyond the corner, and the children had disappeared among the crowd. The music was louder now. People held cigarettes in long, slender holders, and their smoke filled the room. The women's dresses clung to their bodies as they swayed back and forth. Their conversations were nothing more than murmurs over the music that continued to grow louder and louder.

I wavered at the entrance. My gaze flitted past different individuals, but no one turned to look at me. Sweat clung to my skin and trickled down my body.

Someone started screaming, and I noticed the fire wrapping around the curtains and up the ceiling just as everyone else did. Flames caught their clothing, and they panicked and ran. Not one of them touched me in all the frenzy as they pushed past.

I looked down at my hands. Orange tongues of flame licked across them.

When I opened my eyes, the ringing in my ears remained. I was sure I was suffocating. I peeled the tightly tangled sheets from my body. I felt for the thermometer on my bedside table. The ringing formed a pounding headache in my temples.

Even though every object appeared to have a fuzzy edge, I could still make out the numbers, 100.1°F. My eyes were stinging. I closed them again and dropped the thermometer onto my bed.

Should I take sleeping medicine? Did I even want to go back to sleep?

I tried to focus on my breathing and get the pounding in my head to go away when I heard that the ringing was distant from my ears. I sat up at the edge of my bed. My eyes were partly open, and a rush of heat filled my body.

My box of blue pills was at the corner of my nightstand. I

unscrewed the top, dumped two pills, and swallowed them down with the water I had left the night before.

I picked up the phone, and the ringing vibrated in my hand.

"Hello?" I said.

"Hey, I'm just calling to check in on you."

I mumbled some sort of sound of recognition. It was Sally.

"Is everything okay?"

"I just woke up."

"Is that all?"

I bit down on my bottom lip. I felt like crying. *You can cry after you move into your new place,* I thought. *You'll feel better then.*

"Yeah, I have a slight fever. I took medicine, though. It should come down soon."

I could hear Sally sigh on the other side of the line.

"I'm okay," I said, doing my best to be reassuring.

"I know you will be. I just wish that you had someone to help you. If I could be down there with you, I would -"

"I'm okay. How's Louis?"

Sally sighed again.

"He told his teacher today that he didn't do his homework because he had a baseball game last night. He told me that he didn't have any homework. I guess it was stupid of me to trust him, but I want him to feel like he has more independence, you know? I know he's only eight, but I want him to know that he can do stuff on his own. I mean, asking for help whenever he needs it, of course. I don't know, I guess I just wanted to trust him more than anything, but now I'm going to have to check his folders and text his teacher every night to see if he has homework."

"You don't have to do that if you don't want to."

"What do you mean?'

"You could keep one of those sticker charts or something, and every time he does his homework and doesn't lie about it, he gets a sticker. After so many stickers, he gets to do something fun."

"I didn't think of that." There was a pause on the other end. It sounded like Sally was going through a tunnel. She must be driving home. She usually called when she was driving home.

The clock on the nightstand glared in red digits: 6:20. I felt like I was going to throw up. I should call room service after this.

"So, is West Virginia turning out to be what you remembered?"

"I haven't had a lot of time to explore. I think that I went out this morning to the island." I pressed the back of my hand that wasn't holding my phone into my eyes. "I've just been exhausted. I've slept so much and had the strangest dreams."

"Is that an effect of your medicines?"

"It's not supposed to be."

"Are you taking your medicines?"

I almost laughed. Sally had a habit of asking people questions in the same tone one might use with a child. It annoyed some people, but I always thought it was funny.

"Yes, I'm taking my medicines."

"So, when exactly are you moving into your new home?'

"The movers are coming in two days. I'll probably go down at the same time and help them. Even though I haven't been out that much, I can already tell that life is much slower here than it was in Chicago. It's exactly what I needed."

"That's really good. You could have just moved to the rural parts of Illinois so I could still visit you, but I get it. Nostalgia has a rope that it likes to tie around people and drag them in. I just wish that you had more help, though."

"I will be okay. Just taking it one day at a time, you know?"

"Yeah," Sally trailed off. "Hey, I just pulled into my driveway. I'll call you back later, okay? And take care of yourself."

"Okay," I said and hung up when she did.

I put my cell phone down, picked up the hotel phone on the nightstand, and dialed room service.

~

A knock came at the door. It couldn't have been more than five minutes since I ordered. I got up from my bed, walked to the door, and peered through the peephole. There was no one there.

It must have been the kids playing in the hallways.

I turned on the TV, and in the corner, it said the time. Nearing Seven. I needed to take my medicine. My suitcase was by the door. I opened it up and rummaged through it until I found them. Blue and pale green and white pills scattered onto my palm. I walked back to my bed as I started to put them into my mouth. I took my water from the nightstand and washed back the pills.

The knock at the door came again.

I walked back to the door and peered through the peephole. Finally, room service.

"Food delivery," he said.

I opened the door.

"Hello. Dinner delivery for Miss—"

"Yes, thank you," I said and grabbed the tray from him. "Have a good evening."

"You too."

I took the tray to my bed and began to pick off pieces of the food. The air conditioning unit ran under the windows, and the curtains fluttered against the breeze. They danced for a while before I grabbed my notebook and pens from the side of the pillow.

I opened it up to an empty page and wrote, "M. saw a face in the window behind the curtains. It had skin the color of fog on an early November day." I curled further into bed and continued to write while eating my food piece by piece.

The TV droned on in the background, the volume turned so low it was barely a whisper.

~

The sound of horses' hooves clattered against the road. I could not see them through the window, but they were near. Ever the more present was the sound of a baby crying. The child wailed and wailed, and footsteps sounded across the ceiling. I felt someone tug at the bottom of my dress. I looked down to see a little girl in front of me.

She asked if you were a guest. She had an Irish accent. I opened my mouth but couldn't speak. I couldn't breathe. I pulled at the collar of my dress.

"You're warm," she said. "It gets hot here during the summer. I'll fetch you a glass of water."

My dreams only come back to me in fragments.

I watched the waves lap across one another on the sternwheeler ride to Blennerhassett Island. I held my bag close to my side. I only felt a bit nauseous, but I had everything I needed, just in case. We approached the shore and came to a stop. A man was standing on the sand. He was dressed in a loose, cotton shirt underneath his vest, baggy pants that ended just below his knees, and knee-high, white socks with black buckle shoes.

"Hello, hello, oh yes. Why isn't it such a beautiful day? Hello," he said to each of us as we walked off the ship. I was one of the last ones to get off, and we all stood in a group. He stared at us for a minute before saying, "Such a lovely group of people. Alright, well, if you'll just follow me."

I trailed behind the others. The air was getting warmer, but my hands still stung from the cold. I crossed my arms and tucked my hands into my armpits. As I walked, I stared at the grass passing underneath my feet. It was a habit from a childhood filled with clumsy falls. I did look up, though, when the tour guide said, "In front of me, you will see the Blennerhassett Estate."

It was three buildings connected to one another by two

curving walkways. Seeing it reminded me of going to the Greenbrier with my grandparents. I would have to go back there sometime again. I hardly remembered what it looked like; I must have been five years old when I was there last. A child in front of me pulled at the edge of his mom's shirt.

"Mom, is that a castle?" He asked. His mom smiled, and her shoulders heaved up as if she was about to laugh.

"No. It's just a really large house."

"Harman and Margaret Blennerhassett were wealthy Irish aristocrats," our tour guide said as we walked into the mansion's entrance. "They were fleeing political persecution and scandal from their native homeland. They came to America, and eventually, they came to this island, where they decided to settle. They laid out the plans for this building," he said, gesturing to the space around him. "And they had it built for them. Now, it must be noted that this is not the original house that was on the land. In 1805, the Blennerhassetts allowed their estate to become headquarters for Aaron Burr for his military expedition to the Southwest. The Blennerhassetts were well known for their hospitality, but this, let's say 'alliance,' with Aaron Burr and his military would ultimately lead to their downfall."

A little girl in the front raised her hand.

"Yes," the tour guide said while pointing at her.

"Is it the Aaron Burr from *Hamilton?*"

The room burst out into laughter. We started to walk into a next-door room on the left. The room had a fireplace made out of the same dark wood as the floor. The walls were painted mint green, and large windows spanned across them. The natural light from the windows lit up the entire room. There was a writing desk in the corner, and a portrait of a young man hung above the fireplace.

"It was rumored that Aaron Burr wanted to band several states and U.S. territories together to break apart from the United States and form their own country. With Harman Blennerhassett's permission, Aaron Burr used Blennerhassett Island as his headquarters. It was here that he started gaining men for his military and making plans for his attack. There is no historical evidence to back me up on this, but I like to think that this is the study where Aaron Burr was scheming like a madman for his attack." The tour guide smiled, and some of the people from the group laughed.

"Come on, let's go upstairs," he said while he led the group in walking out of the room. We all started to walk up the curving staircase at the entrance of the building.

"Word of Aaron Burr's attack was never meant to reach Thomas Jefferson, but it did. When the President found out, he immediately put a stop to Aaron Burr's plans, and, in the process, this estate was burned to the ground. The Blennerhassetts were forced to flee the island. Harman Blennerhassett was arrested, but he was eventually let go. Quite a few years later, archeologists discovered the remains of this estate. From the pieces they had, they were able to construct a plan for a near-to-exact replica of the original estate. That is what we are standing in right now."

As we passed them, I stared at the curtains hanging by the windows, and I saw flames spreading across the fabric in my mind. I felt sweat start to make my jacket cling to my arms. I took it off and wrapped it around my waist.

"While that tragic event may be the one that the island is the most well known for, it is, unfortunately, only one of the many tragedies that fell upon this island. Fortunately for us, we have medicines and other treatments that help us live longer, happier, and healthier lives. That was not the case during the late 1700s to early 1800s when the Blennerhassetts lived on this island. At times, disease ran rampant through the island, and many children passed away, including some of Margaret Blennerhassett's."

We walked into a bedroom. The walls were a light pink, almost a peach color. The bed was against the wall in the center of the room. It had white blankets and a pearl-colored canopy. A baby doll with blonde, curly hair and a cracked, porcelain face rested on the center of the bed.

"Margaret Blennerhassett did have some children that lived to adulthood."

A child, taking her turn peering into the bedroom, started giggling. She lifted her hand to cover her mouth, but the giggles still escaped her. Her orange, frizzy hair bounced with her laughs. Her mom grabbed her hand and started walking her forward. The little girl waved at something in the room before she left.

Once everyone had walked past the room, I turned back to look inside it once more. There was nothing in there that I could imagine the little girl laughing at.

I walked forward with the rest of the group.

The few people outside had picnics spread out across the lawns. Their voices hung in the air. A couple passed a Frisbee between one another. Chills spread across my skin, and I nearly jumped forward when I heard a child start to laugh. I turned to see her standing beside me. She had orange, frizzy hair, the same child from the tour.

Her mother walked up to her and held out her hand. "Come on, the picnic is ready." When the girl wouldn't listen, she grabbed her child's hand and started to pull her forward.

The girl started to cry out. "Can't I go play with them?"

"Play with who?"

"The kids running through the trees. There," she said and pointed vaguely toward the trees. "They're dressed like the people working here. Please, Mom, they're having so much fun."

"Where?"

The child pointed again at a place where no one was.

The mother sighed. "You can't play with your imaginary

friends now. It's lunchtime." She started walking away with her daughter.

"But they're not imaginary," the daughter mumbled. She dragged her feet lazily against the ground while she let her mother pull her away.

My gaze lingered on the forest the girl had just been staring at. The trees were planted in straight lines. I looked for children, but I didn't see anybody. I sat down on a patch of grass underneath a tree and ate the snacks from my bag. I balanced my notebook on my lap and opened it up to a blank page.

I made my way up to the second floor of the hotel. It was in the late afternoon, and even though I felt well enough, my muscles ached, and every breath I took made my chest feel heavy. It would be so nice to crawl into bed right now.

There was a mirror around the corner. I snuck glimpses of myself each time I passed it. The golden frame with its wilting flowers often took my attention. There was the sound of footsteps running along the hallways, somewhere further behind me. As I turned the corner away from the mirror, I caught my reflection. Cigarette smoke curled behind me. I had never realized that the mirror had cloudy spots all over it. I reached out to touch the mirror, and the smoke formed into the shape of a man.

I turned around. There was no one there. But, as I turned back to the mirror, the shadow remained in its glass. A head was distinctly there. There were even two hollows for its eyes. I could not tell where its arms ended and its body began. A pulsating pain formed in the back of my head. As I breathed in, I felt the sickness creep into my stomach.

Only a trick of the light, I thought. I reached my hand behind me while staring into the mirror. There was nothing there.

A gentle humming rang through my ears.

My touch did nothing to distort the shadow, but my hand remained there. Pinpricks rose across my palm and the back of my hand. It felt like I had submerged my hand in ice water. Then, it felt like my hand was burning.

The sound of ballroom music was muffled underneath my feet.

I felt this once before when I had grabbed onto a hot curling iron. I pulled my hand back, and a swelling blister took up most of my palm.

"You can never escape the cycle, can you, darling?" A man's heavy, gruff voice said into my ear.

I pushed my feet forward. They stumbled over one another, and I fell into the wall. I dragged my hand along the wall, and my body felt like it was falling forward as I ran. The humming in my ears turned to crying as I choked back my own sobs. My room was at the end of the hallway. Shadows wavered at the corners of my vision. I fell against the door. My key fumbled in my hands, and I unlocked it. I turned on my lights. There were no shadows in my room. Nausea rose from my stomach into my throat, and my bag fell from my arm as I ran to the bathroom.

Pieces of my vomit caught in my hair.

My hair, wet from the shower, clung to my puffy face. My breaths choked from my cries, and my vision was blurry. I slid down onto the bathroom floor and wrapped my arms around my knees.

Just breathe. You're just tired. Deep breath in, deep breath out.

I liked to think that there was a higher power, somebody or something, that could take away all of my pain. The summers I had spent with my grandparents were the only times I had gone to church. I wished that there was a God and hoped that He could hear me.

I wanted someone to grab my hand and pull me up like the

mom had done with her child on the island. I wanted them to open my hand and put all of the pills I needed into my palm. I wanted them to put a glass of water into my other hand. I couldn't just put the pills down. I would have to swallow them.

I will feel so much worse if I don't take my medicine.

I was leaving at the end of the day tomorrow. I would start moving into my house by the evening.

I needed to take my medicine.

I pushed myself off of the cold floor. Spots formed across my vision, but I pushed myself up until I stood. As I walked back into my room, I saw my bag of medicine on my bed. I crawled into bed. I remembered leaving my bag by the door, but maybe I left it here this morning. I found the bottles and unscrewed the tops. I poured the pills into my hand and swallowed them back with the water I had left out on my nightstand. For a second, I thought about checking to see if the medicines could make me hallucinate. I turned the description of the side effects to face me. *That is the only reason for everything,* I thought. I placed the container on my nightstand without reading it.

Tomorrow, you need to do something good for yourself, something that will make you smile. I promised this to myself as I closed my eyes and snuggled further into bed.

The walls were painted mint green. Upstairs, they were peach. People were playing cards at the table. They were laughing. Like waves in a storm crashing over one another, notes being played on a piano that was not in tune echoed through the house. Two children ran past me. The boy, who was behind the girl, reached out his hand in their game of tag.

I smiled at them.

When I looked towards the ground, I saw my dress. It was white with green flowers embroidered at the bottom section of the skirt that touched the ground. The children ran and turned a corner, where they were taken away from my sight. *I should leave too*, I thought, and so I picked up my skirt and walked in the opposite direction that the children went.

Two hands grabbed onto my shoulders. A woman turned me to face her. She had swollen, glossy eyes and thin skin wrapped around her delicate bones.

"We never can leave," she said in broken syllables.

The hallway was lit by a faint glow of lamps with dying bulbs. Numbers lined the doors that lined the walls and went on as far as I could see.

I heard the children's footsteps before I saw them. They ran down the hallway. I stumbled after them.

A door creaked open. The children walked into the door at the end of the hallway. They turned around, and their heads peeked out from the side of the door. Each child held a finger up to their lips.

Sweat clung to my arms and neck.

I opened the door. Had I walked to it? I had no recollection of walking at all.

The room was alight in a spectacular orange hue. The fire crept up the walls, to the curtains, and up to the ceiling, where the flames were like the waves in an ocean.

The children were standing at the edge of the bed. They were staring at my body.

The sheets wrapped around my blistering red skin. They were wet and clung to my body.

My breaths were uneven as I opened my eyes. The only light in my room came from the faint glow of the lamp on my nightstand. I breathed in and out and felt the heat pulsating off my skin. The sheets were so heavy. I could barely lift them off my body as I tried to slide to sit on the side of the bed.

I grabbed the thermometer on the edge of my nightstand and stuck it into my mouth. There was a pressure building on my eyes, forcing me to only see the world from narrow slits.

The thermometer beeped.

I took it out of my mouth, and in black lines, it said 102.1°F.

"No," I muttered to myself. My throat felt like it was closing in on itself. *Today was supposed to be a better day.*

A distant ringing came to my ears. I felt for my phone on my nightstand and picked it up.

I wasn't going to answer it, but it was Sally.

"Hey, Julia, just calling to make sure you're okay. Aren't you moving into your new house today?"

"Yeah," I said, and my voice strained on that one word.

"What's wrong?"

The tears streamed down my face before I could wipe them away. I covered my mouth as I tried to breathe in.

"What's wrong, Julia? You're beginning to scare me."

"I feel so sick," I muttered.

"Do you need me to call someone? Your doctor? Shit, I know you gave me her number. Where is it."

"No," I breathed in and out. "I just want to talk for now."

"Okay." There was a pause.

"I had such a good day yesterday. I went to the island. I spent nearly the whole day there, and when I returned, I thought I was okay. I'm never okay anymore, and I'm so tired. I miss being okay. I miss traveling to new places, and I miss how much I used to love life. I feel so useless now." My voice crumbled apart until I could hardly understand what was coming out of my own mouth. "I was so ready for today, but I woke up with a fever. I don't even know if I can leave this room without passing out." I pressed my palms into my eyes and groaned. "God, I sound so ridiculous and stupid. I'm sorry."

"Hey," Sally interrupted. "Never apologize for how you feel. Okay? You contribute so much to this world. You're a great writer. You might not think so, but I've read some of your stuff, and I know you are. You contribute something to this world every time you put pen to paper. Every time you pick up this phone, you contribute something to this world. You are truly my only friend. I don't know what I would do without you."

I felt myself smile. "Louis is not your friend?"

"Louis is my son, and I love him like he's my son, and I love you like you're my friend. It's an important difference. Listen, I don't know what you're going through. I'll never be able to fully understand, but to me, it sounds like you're having a bad day."

A short laugh came out of my mouth. "You could say that. Bad days seem to be my normal now."

"Yes, and you know, I don't mean to make your situation seem less important than it actually is by using the phrase, 'bad day,' but I want you to know that you're not alone. Every single person has things that hold them back from accomplishing everything that they want to accomplish. Usually, it's multiple things that make people have bad days, but there's good in the bad and bad in the good. Do you understand what I'm saying?"

"Kind of."

"Okay, so you're moving in today?"

"Yes."

"What time?"

"It depends when the movers get here."

"Okay, how long does it take for your fever to come down?"

"A couple of hours, more or less, if I rest."

"Okay, so here's what you need to do. You need to take your medicine and then spend the morning resting, watching TV, or doing whatever you need. Treat yourself to a nice lunch or whatever you want to do. Then, you need to pack, set your alarm, and take a nap before you go to your new house to feel better before moving in. Does that sound good?"

"Yeah," I said, and I was actually smiling now. "Thank you. I feel a lot better now."

"Are you sure?"

"Yes."

"Okay, just know that you can call me anytime, especially today. I'm here for you, and take care of yourself."

"I know, and I will. I don't know what I would do without you."

"Same to you."

It was a Tuesday afternoon, and hardly anyone was in the hotel's restaurant. I slept throughout the entire morning. I think that I dreamed only of darkness. I woke up with hunger pains and realized that it was time for lunch. A waitress directed me to a table and gave me the menu. As I sat staring at it, nausea settled in the pit of my stomach. It was nice listening to the people cook in the background. I ordered something light, brought out my notebook, and wrote while waiting for my food.

I was light-headed as I walked back to my room. It was nearing two, and nobody had contacted me about the movers. There was a sign just a few steps away from the restaurant. I hadn't noticed it when I walked in earlier, but it was there, taking up most of the wall closest to me.

It was made out of dark metal – maybe copper painted a darker shade of gray – and was noted as a historical sign at the top. I skimmed through the sentences.

"On the evening of May 9, 1979, a fire broke out on the second floor of the Blennerhassett Hotel. While the fire consumed portions of the hotel, it was extinguished before it could engulf the entire building. The hotel would like to thank the following sponsors who helped to return the hotel to its former glory."

Below the line, there was a list of names. I could barely read as my vision became hazy. The all too familiar sinking feeling returned in the pit of my stomach. My trembling fingers trailed across the wall while I tried to steady them. A faint wave of heat washed over my body. I just needed to get to the elevator.

The light from my window danced through my drawn curtains. It was raining outside, and its reflection created a wave-like pattern across the ceiling. Someone was crying in the distance. I closed my eyes.

The wind whipped around the building. It carried a gentle humming sound. I felt so light as if I was floating.

Floating away from the pain as I fell asleep to the lullaby.

IN THE SILENCE UNTO THEE

They give me gifts.

A flower here, a penny there, all laid out on the stone for me to see. They all could be offerings, but to whom? I am no God. No, I think that they want something back.

This is usually what one does: exchange a present for another with other people. It is a way of human nature. I know this because, when I peer into their eyes, it is what their souls are telling me that they want.

Soul is not quite the right word for it, but it is close enough that it will do.

They whisper into my ear what they want in return. Sometimes, it's so cold that I can barely hear them. So many different wishes; to have time off for a vacation, to get a good grade on an exam, to find work, to mend a relationship, to be able to pass down life, and it only goes on.

I know as little of the world's workings as they do, but I pray to the universe for them as they pray to me. Perhaps there is something in my prayers because they always come back.

I leave the hateful ones to their own prayers. The colors around them burn a bright red when someone wishes for evil. Sometimes, I hear what they have done through the cries and screams of the people laid to rest, but usually, I can only see the color. The rest is silence.

I have my own little tricks, though. Sometimes, a person will trip and fall. Others will have their clothes unbutton. Harmless mishaps. Nothing more, but they are still efforts to make that red a little more dull.

As they walk through the cemetery, they admire me. They come, and they go. The years pass and moss still grows over me, and the rain soaks the stones. They still come to me, though.

They pass through the gates, and they come to look at me. But, when those gates are shut, and the stars sprinkle over the sky, my limbs tingle until I stretch out my fingers and lift my arms up from the stone.

The moonlight is warm against my body. The crickets sing the rest of the animals to sleep.

I have heard the rumors. They think they hear me crying at night for the souls lost in the war between the North and the South. It can't be me, though. I cannot cry. It has to be another.

Within the veil of darkness, I stretch out my stiff muscles and reach to the sky. One step forward, two steps back. I trace through the grass and the graves, and I dance. My fingers try to wrap around the moon through all of her changes. Oh, if only I could reach her!

I reach for someone else instead.

There is a man who dances with the moon and me. He wears a black coat that waves when we move. He has hands that hold mine, but he does not have a face. When we dance, I look out toward the stars.

He has no colors surrounding him, no mumblings of a soul. He must enjoy our time together, though, since in the first moments after leaving my pedestal, he is always by my side. I do not know where he comes from, but he has never missed a dance.

Exhaustion only comes to me as the sky turns to the lighter blue of the morning. It is then that the man in the black coat bows to me, and I return to my pedestal.

It does get lonely sometimes. I suppose that is why I hold my sullen expression for as long as I do.

I often imagine running away with the visitors who bring me gifts, but it would be futile. I cannot move any of my limbs in the sunlight, despite how I try. They are fascinated whenever my hands move positions, even though, most of the time, the movement is nothing more than an illusion in their own minds. Imagine what their faces would look like if they saw me in the night!

I have dreamed of leaving some night, but where would I go? To another cemetery, only to find loneliness there as well?

There is loneliness everywhere in this world. The wishes remind me every day.

The man in the black coat always comes to me when thoughts of escape enter my mind. We only ever share our dance, and with that dance, he makes everything less lonely. I do not remember what came before or if I have always existed. I do not know how I will end, but everything on this Earth must end eventually.

For now, though, I dance through the night. When morning arrives, I take my place at the stone. I drape my hands over the scroll and hold my eyes open to see who visits. Sometimes, I hold my mouth open to scream, but nobody hears me.

THE LIGHT IN THE DARKNESS

Teddy and Patrick weren't supposed to be out this late on the railroad tracks. They weren't rebellious children, no, just curious. Patrick's papa told them about Screaming Jenny. He told them, while they sat out on the front porch and the mosquitos were starting to come out into the summer, that Jenny was a poor girl who lived near the railroad tracks a long time ago. She was cooking herself dinner one night and trying to keep warm by the stove. Well, she got too close to the stove, and went up in flames. She ran outside to the railroad tracks, screaming for help, but she was dead and gone when the fire overtook her. Patrick's papa had said that he and his friends used to walk along those railroad tracks when he was a young boy, looking for the ghost of Screaming Jenny.

"Did you ever find her?" Teddy had asked. His cheeks were a bright red. He always got sunburnt when the summer months were starting up, and school was ending.

Patrick's papa shook his head. "We did hear her screaming once, though."

"What did she sound like?"

Patrick's papa scrunched up his face like he had smelled something awful. "The worst sound you could ever imagine. Do you remember when you," he pointed to Teddy, "broke your leg, and you were hollering so badly that the whole town could hear you?"

Both Teddy and Patrick nodded. It was, after all, the reason why Teddy was called Teddy. After he broke his leg, he carried a Teddy Bear with him everywhere he went.

"Well, it was like that, but as loud as an oncoming train when you're standing right next to the railroad tracks. I near about fell over from the sound."

"What did you do after that?"

"We ran for our lives. We were sure of one thing at that

moment: we did not want to meet the thing that made that sound.”

Patrick and Teddy were not convinced as they walked along the train tracks after school to find the truth of Screaming Jenny. The tracks went on forever. The two boys had handfuls of broken pieces of rocks that they would throw into the distance and listen to clink against the metal as they fell.

As the air grew cooler around them and the once bright blue sky was settling into a light pink for the sunset, Patrick had a sinking feeling in the pit of his stomach.

“I think we should go back.”

“No way,” Teddy said. “We came all this way, and Screaming Jenny only comes out at night. We don’t want to miss her.”

“But we’re going too far. We won’t get back home until morning at this rate. We’re going to be in so much trouble,” Patrick grumbled.

Teddy didn’t turn back to look at Patrick. He just kept walking forward. “I’ll tell my parents that I spent the night at your house, and you’ll tell your parents that you spent the night at mine.”

“Don’t you think our parents will call each other?”

Teddy threw a pebble into the distance. “Nah.”

“We need to go back.”

“Stop being such a crybaby. We’ll go back after we see Screaming Jenny.”

Teddy had barely finished speaking when a low rumbling came from the Earth, followed by the sound of somebody trying to catch hold of his breath.

Teddy turned towards Patrick and smiled. “I told you she would be here,” he said, but only Patrick could see what was behind him.

It was nothing more than a speck on the horizon at this point, but it was there. A train, making its way across the tracks faster than Patrick had ever thought a train could go.

The train’s detonator went off.

Patrick tried to yell out Teddy's name, but the sound was lost to the mountains. Teddy saw his friend's mouth moving, and he had heard the detonator. A brush of cold air went through him as he turned back around. The train cars waved back and forth as if nothing more than a string was holding them together.

Something invisible struck Teddy. Everything in him told him to move away, but he couldn't seem to lift so much as a finger. In the corner of his vision, he saw something orange and bright.

Patrick was the one who saw the outline first. It was a woman. She flailed around as flames licked up her long hair and limbs.

Teddy, unable to move so much as his neck, saw the first wheels on the train explode until fragments of what it once was scattered along the tracks.

The detonator went off again, and then the sound died.

Jenny opened her mouth and let out a scream that brought warm blood trickling down Patrick's ears.

He touched the side of his face and brought his hand up close to his eyes. In front of him stood Teddy. He looked past the red on his fingertips to the blurry outline of his friend.

Patrick found enough strength to run forward and push his friend off of the railroad tracks.

The train continued moving forward. As it did so, the light around Patrick and Teddy diminished, surrounding them in darkness.

THEY COME TO US WHILE WE ARE SLEEPING

~ THE DREAM ~

The little girl smiled at me. She picked up the ends of her dress and started spinning. Her shadow, curving like a winding staircase, followed her in the darkening room. She stumbled and stopped, facing me. Her body had the length and curves of a young adult now.

A man with welts, burned and puckered across his throat, walked up next to her. She laced her fingers through his.

"Why did you do this?" He asked.

"Follow me," she said.

They said the two phrases simultaneously, and their voices blended, masking which words originated from whom.

I saw only darkness as I opened my eyes. I listened to John snoring beside me. I reached across and shook him awake.

"Mmh, what is it?" He flipped onto his other side to face me, but his face was still buried in the pillow.

He tried to reach out his arm and wrap it around me, but it hit my chin. I moved his hand away.

"Sorry."

"It's okay," I mumbled. "John, we can't go to the caves today."

"Mmh?"

"I had a dream—"

"Go back to sleep," he said, pushing himself further underneath the blankets. "Tell me about it in the morning."

I stared up at that ceiling for most of the night. I closed my eyes, only to open them a couple of hours later.

~DEPARTURE~

"It was just a nightmare," John said. I passed him a handful of granola bars, and he shoved them into the backpack.

"I know," I said. "But I've never had a dream like this one. My dreams are always like high fantasy movies with a low budget for special effects." John snickered and started to fill up the water bottles.

"Maybe you've had realistic dreams before; you just don't remember them."

"I would've remembered those."

"Maybe you didn't. I hardly ever remember my dreams. Just think about it. It makes sense that you would have a nightmare. You're probably nervous, even if you don't realize it."

I zipped up my backpack. "Did you get everything?" I asked.

"For an hour and a half, self-guided tour, I have three days worth of food, water, and medical emergency kits for us both," John said. He was trying to smile for my benefit, but when he saw that I couldn't match his smile, he shook his head like I was a child who wouldn't listen to his suggestions.

"Did you get the sleeping bags?"

"We're only spending a little bit over an hour there."

"What if we get lost?"

"We won't. The workers time us from the moment we walk in and send people to look for us if we don't return in time. Besides, the sleeping bags will just weigh us down. You're worrying too much," he said as we both put our backpacks and supplies into the car's back seat.

"I just have this feeling. My heart won't stop racing. It happens whenever I get sleep paralysis. It feels like I'm going to throw up." We closed the back doors and opened the front ones.

"You're freaking yourself out. Do you really think the owners would allow people to go on self-guided tours of the caves if there was any danger? They don't want a lawsuit."

The gravel crumbled against the moving tires on the driveway.

"You're right; I just can't get rid of this feeling."

"You're just nervous. You liked exploring the caves in Tennessee."

"I know. This is different, though." John grabbed my hand, and I laced my fingers through his.

"We're going to be fine. Just have fun. I'll make a promise to you."

"What's that?"

"We'll only go to the parts of the cave that you want to go to."

I shook my head. "That's not a good promise."

"Why not?"

"Because you're the one who has explored this cave before. I know nothing about it. I'll be the one who gets us lost."

"We'll be fine."

And because I couldn't think of anything else to say, I said, "Okay." I held onto the bottom of my seat as we turned around the corner.

"Hey, you know what Greenbrier County is most famous for?"

"The Greenbrier."

"Yes, but I meant ghost stories."

I shook my head, and John saw it from the corner of his eye.

"What?"

"You always tell ghost stories when you're trying to distract me."

He sighed. "Yeah, but it usually works."

I nodded, "Go ahead then."

"Do you know of the Greenbrier Ghost?" The corners of his mouth lifted up.

"Never heard of it."

"Well, there are many versions of the story, but the one I've heard most often was about a woman who was in love with a man in her village. She wanted to marry this man more than anything, but her family begged her not to, especially her mother. She had this bad feeling about the guy, you know?"

"Like the bad feeling I have about today?"

He gave me a side-eye. "This was about a person, not a place. It was different."

"Not so different."

"Do you want to hear the rest of the story?"

I waved my hand forward. "Continue."

"Aside from their feelings, her family didn't have anything to convince her not to marry the man. Clean record and everything. Well, long story short, she died shortly after the marriage. It was customary during this time for the women to wash the body of a recently deceased in their village, but the husband wouldn't allow this. He said that he was grieving, and to get over his grief, he needed to wash his wife's body, prepare her for the funeral, and bury her. Nobody suspected anything except for the mother of the girl who died. She knew that something was wrong. Still, she didn't have any proof until her daughter came to her in a dream one night and professed that her husband had killed her."

I tried to seal my lips together, but laughter still spilled out.

"Don't laugh. This was the proof that the mother had been waiting for. They dug up her daughter's body and found red marks covering her throat. She had been strangled to death by her husband."

I took a deep breath, and my laughter settled down.

"Is that why you want me to go to this cave so badly? So you can strangle me to death?"

"Of course not."

"You better not, or else I'll go to my mom in a dream and tell her what happened."

"You're ridiculous."

"Lots of things happen," I said.

"What does that mean?"

But we both burst into laughter as we turned the corner onto a dirt road.

-ARRIVAL-

The air was as heavy as the wind after a thunderstorm inside the cave.

"We must stay on the path the whole time," I said. "That's what she told me. If we're not back eventually, they send people out looking for us."

"You know, we never had these paths growing up, and nobody got lost."

"I trust the paths more than I trust your memory."

"My memory is adequate."

"And the paths are certain."

We laughed, and I felt John stand closer to me as the path narrowed. Water dripped down from the stalactites, and the sound of it hitting the floor echoed across the caves. A couple was talking behind us. I could barely make out what they were saying. When I turned to look back at them, they looked directly at me, their mouths still moving. I turned away.

Breathe in, breathe out. My shoulders relaxed a bit.

~TIME ESCAPES WHILE WALKING~

"How do you know when we're supposed to be back?" I asked. Silence and our footsteps had filled my ears for the past few minutes. When I asked John the question, it looked like I was waking him up from a dream.

"I, um, set a timer," he said. "Do you want me to check to see how much time we have left?"

"No. I was just wondering if you did something to know when we're finished. We'll know once we hear it go off. I'm kind of bored, though, aren't you?"

"Let's play a game, then."

I shook my head.

"Come on," he begged.

"What kind of game?"

"I Spy."

"You have to be kidding me," I groaned

"What? I Spy is a great game."

"Uh, let me guess, I spy something brown. Could it be, I don't know, rocks?"

John sighed. "Fine, what game do you want to play?"

"Tell me about what it was like to grow up here."

He glared at me. "That's not a game."

"Yeah, but I'd like to know. I grew up surrounded by people. Here, I mean, not just in this cave but everywhere in this town, you have so much space. You could spend the whole day outside and not see your neighbors."

He laughed. "Yeah, I guess it was nice that way. There's not much to say, though."

"Everyone has a story."

"Yeah, I guess so. Well, I spent most of my childhood playing outside."

"That's a given."

He rolled his eyes. "It's different here, though, in the

mountains. No matter how far away I was from my house, I never got caught in a storm. You can feel it in the air before it's about to rain or snow. It's the most incredible feeling, right before a thunderstorm. It reminds you that you're alive. If some of my friends and I were too far away from our house and it was about to storm, we would find a cave to hide in until the storm cleared. I know it makes us sound like true hillbillies out here, seeking shelter in the caves."

"No, it doesn't. It sounds like fun."

"It was fun. We had this game that we liked to play called 'explorers.' Creative, right? We were eight."

"What was the game like?"

"Well, there were a lot of elements to it, but it mainly centered on things that we could find. Bird feathers, empty turtle shells, stuff like that. Everything that we found, we would gather it all together and put it in our secret hiding spots. Mine was a hole by my house that I covered with fallen leaves. We would pretend to have fortresses by the hiding spots, but these fortresses usually meant we had to stick by our hiding spots. We would use sticks to try and attack people who came to steal our stuff. We would pretend that the sticks were swords. It was an ongoing game where we always tried to protect the stuff in our hiding spots because whoever had the most stolen stuff was considered the king. We all wanted to be the king."

"I wish that I had your childhood. At eight, my sister and I used to get in trouble if we played hide and seek in the apartment building."

"Yeah. My parents probably should have been more cautious about where we went and how long we were gone. We used to stay out all day, from sunrise until sunset, without seeing our parents."

"Wow. Not even for meals?"

"We would go inside and make our own meals. Our parents usually weren't there. Sometimes they were, but not often. I don't know where they were."

"Nature really was your second home, wasn't it?"

John shrugged. "I spent more time outside than I did inside. I was a hyper kid, though. It wouldn't have been good for me to stay inside."

I grabbed my water bottle from the side of my backpack.

Have we been down here for longer than an hour? What if we went into a part of the cave that we weren't supposed to go into, and they won't be able to find us? I thought, but I tried to reassure myself. *We've been going in mostly a straight line since we got here.*

For a second, I debated on telling my thoughts to John, but he would think my anxiety was useless like he had before we got here. *It probably was useless.*

Instead, I asked, "How much longer does your timer say? I feel like we've been down here for a long time." I took a drink from my water and put it back in my backpack. "I would have guessed you would stay down here for hours if you could," I teased.

"Maybe, but I don't want them to send a team to come looking for us if there's no reason for them to." He said. He pulled the phone out of his pocket. He frowned at the screen, then pressed his thumb into the home button, unlocking it.

"What is it?"

"The timer stopped. I don't know why. Sometimes phones do weird things in caves. There's a science behind it. Something to do with magnetic fields, I think. I'm not sure. We should probably start heading back, just in case."

"Yeah," I said. As we turned around, there was nobody on the walkway with us. "Was there another side walkway attached to this one that we could have taken?"

"I don't think so, but maybe. Why?"

"There was a couple walking behind us for a really long time. They were talking for a while, but then they were quiet. I thought I heard their footsteps. Didn't you hear them?"

"No, but I must not have been paying attention. There probably was another pathway connected to this one, then. They couldn't have vanished into thin air," John replied. I agreed and wrapped my arms across my chest. My hands were shaking. I tucked them against my chest even tighter. My vision was cloudy.

"Can you get me a granola bar?"

"Yeah, um…" John moved his backpack to the front of him. He took out two granola bars. "We've been in this cave for a long time, haven't we? I'm hungry too."

"It could just be the walking. I really don't think that it's been too long. I feel like we started walking only minutes ago."

Children's laughter and footsteps running across the ground clattered around us.

"See, we're not too far. There are people ahead." As we continued to walk, I heard the laughter only every so often. I began to count. *One, two, three, four. Laughter. One, two, three, four. Laughter.*

It was aligned with our every four footsteps. At step three, I stopped walking, and the laughter died away. My vision pulsated around me.

"Can we sit down for a few minutes? I feel dizzy."

"Yeah," John said, and he moved to sit down next to me.

I brought my knees up to my chest and placed my elbows on them. I held my head in my hands. A wave of heat washed over me and then drained itself from my body. It left my skin tingling.

"Hey, Ruth, can I have your phone?"

"Hmm? Yeah." I rested my head in one of my hands and used my other hand to get out my phone and give it to John.

"How is that possible?" He gasped.

"What?" I hadn't lifted my head, and my eyes were still closed.

"My phone says that it's midnight. Yours says that it's five past four in the morning."

"Didn't you say that phones can do weird things in caves sometimes?"

"Yeah, at least, I think that they can."

"It has to be a weird thing, then. It can't be that late. We would have started to feel hungry, tired, whatever, you know?"

"Yeah. Something feels wrong."

I lifted my head up and opened my eyes. The world stayed still around me. "Let's leave."

"Are you sure you feel up to it?"

"Yeah," I said. John got up before me, and I grabbed onto his hands so he could help me up to my feet. We started walking forward, and I let my hand dangle by my side. My fingers searched for the railing to hold onto, but I touched nothing but empty space.

"Where did the railing go?"

"What railing?"

"There was a railing right here," I waved at the empty space on my right side. "It was here the entire time we were walking."

"It's probably up ahead. Maybe it ended, and you weren't paying attention."

I shook my head. "It was here. Are we still on the same path?"

"Ruth, we have to be on the same path. We've been walking straight ahead this whole time."

"It's just weird."

John started walking slightly faster. "I know. That's why we're getting out of this cave."

Only the sounds of our footsteps surrounded us in the empty space. The silence brought chills to the back of my neck.

"Tell me another story," I said.

"What?"

"Something to distract us until we get out of this cave."

"I don't know any stories."

"You always have a story to tell."

"Why don't *you* tell a story?"

"Because you have better ones."

He held up his hand and tilted his head to the side. I stopped walking as he did, but the footsteps continued to echo. I turned back, but no one was behind us. The edges of my vision were clouded with black spots. As I turned to look forward, I saw a shadow on the cave wall. It was walking in front of us, but nobody was attached to it.

"We need to keep walking," I whispered. John nodded.

Our footsteps created a steady *thrum, thrum, thrum* on the ground. There was another pair of footsteps behind our own. It fell out of sync with ours as we moved faster.

I turned to look back, and I slammed into something.

A man looked down at me. His jaw opened and closed. As it did, he puckered and closed his lips but spoke no words. He walked closer to me in front of the light. I stumbled back.

It was John.

But John was behind him, running towards me.

They both opened their mouths and echoed each other's words: "What happened?"

I lifted my hand and pointed a finger at him that wasn't him.

His fingers dug into my skin. "What's wrong?"

I looked down at his hand wrapped across my arm, but when I looked back up, there was only John. "Ruth, we need to get out of here." He jolted me forward, and I started walking with him.

"You were right there," I said.

He turned back at me, his brow furrowed. "Ruth, I've been here the whole time."

"But it wasn't you."

He opened his mouth to say something and then sealed his lips. Instead, he said, "Let's just get out of here."

~CROSSROADS~

We had to be closer to the entrance now. We had been walking for so long. My legs were tingling, and my stomach growled, but I didn't grab another granola bar. There was no outpouring of light from the entrance, but it had to be close. Just a few more steps. Up ahead, the pathway we were on split into two paths.

"Shit."

"Just keep going straight," John said. "That's what we've been doing this whole time."

"What if we went the other way and didn't see this other pathway because of this rock between them?"

"I don't know," John sighed and wiped his hand over his face. "I think that we went straight."

"John, I think that we should stop moving."

"We have to get out of here, Ruth."

"It feels like we've been down here for more than an hour and a half, which means they must have already sent the rescue team out for us."

"What if that was all just a load of shit? What if they just told us that so we would feel safe?"

"Well, they'll have to send a team out to find us eventually."

"Eventually could be a week or more before they find us. We don't have enough water to last us for anything past three days."

"We do if we stay here and stop moving. If we're lost, we need to stay in one place so it'll be easier for them to find us."

"We can't be lost. We've been walking on this same pathway the whole time."

"I think that we should stay here until they find us."

"But what if we're close to the entrance?"

"What if we're not? The team will know how to get us out of here. It's better to wait for them."

"Okay," John mumbled. He took off his backpack, sat down,

crossed his arms over his knees, and rested his head in them. I sat down next to him.

"Ruth?"

"Yeah?" I turned to him, but he didn't look at me.

"We're not going to another cave for a long time."

"I could die happy if I never went to another cave again," I said. John sighed, and all was quiet around us. I took my phone out of my pocket. There was a notification on the lock screen. A voicemail from my mom.

"I'm so sorry," he said.

"For what?" I asked while I unlocked my phone.

"You didn't want to go here today, and I made you. I should have listened to you."

"My mom left me a voicemail."

"What?" John lifted his head and looked at me. "Can you play it?" I tapped the voicemail. I let out a breath when I heard my mom's voice.

"Hi, honey. I was just calling to make sure that you're okay and all. I don't know if you're back from your cave adventure yet, but please call me when you are. Last night, I had a bad dream about you in the cave, but it was probably nothing. You know how nervous caves make me. Anyway, please call me back when you can. Love you. Bye."

The phone fell as my hands started to shake. There was no sound of it hitting the ground, though. In the corner of my vision, I saw John grab it before it could. He tapped the message to call her, but there was only beeping on our end. Then, all went quiet.

"I don't think we should stay here," John said.

"Then what should we do?"

John gestured down the pathway. "One of us walks down this path, and the other walks down that path. Whoever gets out will get help to find the one who is still in the cave." A heaviness settled around me.

"Okay. I don't have enough food and water, though."

He nodded and opened his backpack. I did the same. We began counting and distributing everything we had until we had the same amount of everything.

~SEPARATE WAYS~

The railing was on my left side down this pathway. When I had walked into the cave, the railing had been on my left side, so it should be on my right now. But it was there, and that was more than I could say of what I saw of John's path.

I started to hum to myself. A quiet sound, just barely louder than my footsteps. "Hey, baby, do you know what that's worth? Ooo, Heaven is a place on Earth." It was a song I listened to years ago. I didn't know if that was even how it went, but it felt right.

"I like your song."

I stiffened and turned to where the voice had come from. A child was sitting on the railing. My fingernails dug into the skin of my palm. She had the same black, straight hair as me and my blue eyes. She was wearing the white dress with lace around the waist that I had loved as a child.

She jumped down from the railing and lifted one hand to cover the laughter coming from her mouth.

"Catch me if you can!" She laughed and ran forward. My feet dragged across the floor as I started to chase after her. I was pushing myself forward, but it felt like someone was holding me back.

Isn't this cave better than the apartment?

It was a thought from my mind, but the voice inside my head was that of the child. Her laughter echoed around me. She would twirl, and her feet would stumble over one another, and then she would begin to run again. No matter how much she stopped, I stayed behind her. I followed her around the corner. Once I stopped, I saw she was standing in the center of an open space.

A smile spread across her face, and her eyes were wide and empty.

"You're never getting out of here," she said and started running again. I reached out my hand, but she remained too far away for me to grab onto her.

Then she stopped, and my fingers wrapped around her shoulder. She didn't turn back to face me, but past her shoulder was John. He was crouching on the floor, passing things out from a box onto the ground.

"It's all my stuff from the secret hiding spot," John said. My hand fell back to my side.

"It's not me!" I screamed, but John never looked up.

"All of my stuff from the game I used to play as a kid." He laughed. "I know it is because of this card from a Cracker Jack box I had. I signed it. I don't remember why, but I did. Here it is!"

She walked forward. I moved in front of her, but she walked past me.

"It's not me, John!" I yelled as loud as I could until I felt the rawness in my throat. He continued to stare at the ground.

"How is this all here?"

She was dragging her feet against the ground, moving slowly, almost as if she enjoyed these seconds spanning out into the next. I ran to John and crouched in front of him. I reached up my hands and tried to shake him, but he wouldn't move. I thought he was staring at me for a brief second, but he was looking up at her.

"You've been right this whole time," he said. "We should have never come here."

"John, that's not me, okay? We need to get out of here."

"Did you find the entrance?" He asked her.

And she smiled at him with those eyes that spoke no feeling. He stood up to meet her, and as soon as I looked up, her hands were around his throat.

She lifted him up to the air. He tried to push her away and scratch her arms, but she continued to hold on.

I got up to my feet and moved to the side, then I ran into her side with all my weight. I saw a glint of silver light against the cave walls. There was a knife in the pile of John's things. Her gaze hadn't moved to watch me as I picked up the knife and grabbed a rock in my other hand.

John fell limp in her arms.

I walked behind her. She had to have seen me in the corner of her eye, but she didn't move. I stabbed the knife into the center of her back and slammed the rock against the side of her head.

John fell between her hands and crumpled to the ground.

The knife and the rock slipped through my fingers as I ran to him.

There was a tint of blue under his pale skin.

He wasn't moving.

I felt for his pulse, but I couldn't feel anything. *He could still be alive,* I thought. My heartbeat pounded into my fingertips.

My arm started to sting. I looked down and watched blood trickle down my arm and onto the ground. The knife swiped past my face.

"Catch you if I can," she said and lunged at me. I scrambled to my feet. The blade slashed against my shoulder as I started to run forward. I turned around the corner. Her laughter jumped across the walls and made my throat feel tight. The world became nothing more than black and white spots. Our footsteps clapped against the floor. Hers were barely out of sync with my own.

Another corner to turn around, and I heard the slick sound of me falling. The world was no longer underneath my feet. A *crack* reverberated in the back of my head. I tried to push myself up, but white light blinded my vision and paralyzed me.

I screamed, and the fire moved from my throat to the back of my head and forced me to shut my mouth.

The laughter stopped.

As my vision came back, I saw the outline of her standing above me. She dangled the knife from her fingertips, right in front of my eyes.

She stood up, and the knife fell.

I closed my eyes, but something clattered next to me.

When I opened my eyes again, she crouched before me. She

started to trace the lines around my nose and cheeks with her fingers before her fingertips landed before my eyes.

"Time to go to sleep," she said, forcing my eyelids closed.

~THE DREAM~

Ruth's body was found first. The team took five minutes to walk into the cave to find her. She was so close to the entrance; if only she hadn't slipped.

They tried to cover up her body as they took her out of the cave. The sheet must have slipped when they were walking, though, because her mother was standing by the entrance and saw the red marks on her skin. She fell to her knees and started crying.

"That bastard," she said. "He killed her. I know it."

She mumbled fragments about the dream, and the people standing by did their best not to listen.

PAPA DOC

The cereal crumbled apart in the vodka, creating a golden mush in the silver of the spoon that Papa Doc shoved with shaking hands into his mouth.

There was a sound like gunshots echoing down the hall, one after the other.

The spoon clattered into the bowl. Papa Doc stood up from his chair and walked towards the door. The world pulsed around him, darkening in the corners of his vision.

"Papa Doc, are you in there?" A man cried out from the other side.

"I'm coming," Papa Doc grumbled.

"Oh God, oh man, you know Huck? He's hurt something—"

Papa Doc opened the door. There were four men outside. Blood covered their hands and reached up past their elbows. In their hands, they held onto Huck.

His shirt, stained red, clung to his body. The lower part of one of his legs dangled just below his knee, only remaining attached by a piece of flesh. A gash tore from his shoulder, across his chest, to his stomach.

All the while Papa Doc was looking at him, he mumbled something incoherent and moved his head side to side.

"We found him past the railroad tracks this morning."

"Must have been drunk and got hit by a train last night," Papa Doc said. "Bring him in." He started to move away. "You can lay him on the table there."

He went to the fireplace and grabbed onto the black handle of the bag that held all his supplies. The handle slipped through his shaking hand.

"Hold on, let me take my highball," he told the boys, who crowded around their friend lying on the table.

The liquid spilled over the kitchen table. His trembling fingers screwed the cap back on, and the bottle fell and rolled to the center as it met the table.

He brought the cup to his lips, and the liquor burned down his throat. His fingers clenched into his palm before he released them.

"Papa Doc, you almost done there?'

"Yeah," he said as he took the first steps away from the kitchen. "When did you find him?"

"Just this morning, past the train tracks. Oh God, do you think he'll live? He has a daughter back home who will miss him."

"Well," Papa Doc said as he looked down at his hands. They were shaking only ever so slightly now. "Let's see what I can do."

He found his bag near the table that the body was lying on. He opened it up – his hands were steady – and he took out a needle and some sutures.

"Don't you think he needs something to bite down on first, Doc?"

Papa Doc looked at the man who had asked him that question. It was James. James had teeth that were so crooked that they crossed over one another. Papa Doc had pulled four of his baby teeth out when he was so young that he had hardly reached Papa Doc's waist. That was when Papa Doc had first moved to Thurmond, West Virginia. James was taller than him now.

"Papa Doc?"

"Hmmm? Yes, I mean, if you can keep something in his mouth, go right ahead."

As they looked around to find something, Papa Doc leaned over Huck's stomach and put the first suture into his skin. Huck leaned up, barely, and cried out. His friends held onto his shoulders and arms to hold him down.

"Isn't there anything you can give him, Papa Doc?"

Papa Doc looked up at James. "I have some liquor in the kitchen, but I have to be honest with you; I don't think Huck can . take it without choking. Just hold him down, will you? While I finish."

Huck's friends nodded, and Papa Doc began to thread the needle through his skin.

"Do you think there's any chance he'll come out of this whole, Papa Doc?"

Papa Doc raised his eyebrows but didn't turn to look at the man speaking next to him. "Well, if he comes out of this at all, he'll be a very lucky fellow. Yes, very lucky. But he won't come out of this whole, no. I'll have to amputate his leg there."

"You'll have to do what?"

Another suture through the skin, and Huck winced. The cloth they had bundled up and put into his mouth muffled his cries.

"I'll have to amputate his leg. There's no use in trying to save it. It's already useless."

"And when do you plan on doing that?" Fred asked.

"Well, I'm hoping that Huck will pass out soon, and I can do it then."

"I'm going to be sick," James said underneath his breath. Papa Doc looked up at him briefly. He was staring at Huck's leg. It was only attached to his body by a piece of skin at the side of his knee. James' face was as pale as a sheet.

"You can step outside," Papa Doc said. James was up and left the room faster than Papa Doc could turn his head to watch him leave.

"It could have been any one of us," Doug said. He was holding onto Huck's head. "We all go down there to play cards and poker, and we all drink more than we should. It could have been any one of us."

Papa Doc threaded the sutures through like he was slicing a knife across butter.

"But Papa Doc gets lots of people who stumble onto the train tracks while drunk, don't you, Papa Doc?"

When Papa Doc looked up, everyone was staring at him. He gave a slight nod and then went back to his work.

"Oh, thank God," Doug said. "That means he really will live."

"It's not a guarantee," Papa Doc muttered. Huck's breaths became ever more shallow under Papa Doc's hands.

"Oh, God, I think he might be dying."

Papa Doc dropped the suture onto Huck's stomach. "Hold that glass up to his lips," he said while pointing toward the table by Doug. Doug grabbed the glass and held it up to Huck's lips.

"Is it foggy?"

"Yes, barely."

"That's good. He's not dead then; he just passed out. I'm going to remove his leg now." Papa Doc found his bag underneath the table. He pulled out the handsaw from it.

"Now, you guys don't have to look, okay? But please, keep him still."

They nodded. Ted was the only one who kept his eyes open and didn't look down.

As Papa Doc brought the handsaw to Huck's skin, James' voice carried from the room's entrance.

"Hey, Papa Doc, do you always keep babies in jars in your hallway?"

"What?" Papa Doc questioned as he released the blade's pressure from Huck's skin.

"The babies in the jars. The dead ones in your hallways; I was wondering why you had them there?" He scoffed. "Are they some sort of trophy or something that you had to hide away? I wouldn't have noticed them if I hadn't bumped into the cabinet. I was afraid I broke something."

"Oh," Papa Doc looked up to meet James' gaze. For a brief moment, he thought of confronting James about wandering around his house when he should have gone out for some fresh air, but he saw James' clenched fists that he pressed tightly against his sides and, instead, said, "Sometimes women lose their babies before birth. They don't know what to do with them, so they give them to me after visiting me to see if anything's wrong with them."

Papa Doc turned back to Huck and brought the handsaw to his leg.

"Oh, is that all?"

He relieved the handsaw from Huck's flesh. "Yes, that's all."

"You see, I don't know any woman who wouldn't want to bury her baby."

"They didn't give birth to them; they miscarried. James, please, help hold down your friend."

"No, I don't think that you're telling the whole truth. Do you know Eleanor?"

Papa Doc turned back and stared at James. Eleanor was a shy girl who always looked away when someone looked directly at her. He hadn't heard much about her in the past couple of years, only rumors around town that she would be graduating top of her class.

"Yes, I know, Eleanor."

James nodded, his hands remaining gripped by his sides. "Well, you see, Eleanor and I have been getting on pretty well. We've been together for well, almost a year now, and we've even talked about getting married and moving in together after we graduate."

"James, we can discuss this after I finish fixing up your friend."

"No, I think that you need to hear this now."

The handsaw clattered to the floor as James began to walk towards Papa Doc.

"Eleanor and I got on so well that she was carrying my child for a while. Only her and I knew; nobody else. Like I said, we were planning on getting married soon, so it was all right. Except, Eleanor didn't think so. She was scared of what her old man would think. Even though I had gotten a job to support us, she was still afraid I would abandon her. I would never abandon her; still haven't to this day." James took a few more steps forward, and Papa Doc remained crouched over Huck's leg.

"Well, one day Eleanor was making a big fuss over the baby, and the next day she wasn't. She wasn't even Eleanor after that. She was empty. I could poke her shoulder with my finger and she would fall over. I knew something was wrong, and so I begged her to tell me what had happened. She wouldn't say anything for a while. God, she was so silent. I begged for a really long time, and, finally, she told me. She said that there wasn't a baby anymore. Well, as you could probably guess, I was confused. I begged her again to tell me what she meant, how it had all happened, and she fell back into that silence. She began to speak in fragments, though, and I pieced those fragments together. She said there wasn't a baby anymore, and we didn't have to worry any longer because she had taken care of it. That's all I could get out of her. I still didn't know what had happened to her until I walked down your hallway and saw those babies you keep in those glass jars. I couldn't help but think to myself. What if one of those was my child?" James paused for a second. "Now, I want you to answer me honestly. Did you take Eleanor's baby out of her?"

James was standing right in front of Papa Doc, so Papa Doc had to look up at him when he said, "I haven't seen Eleanor since she had the flu a couple of winters back. Whatever happened to the baby, she did it herself."

James made a fist and brought it up to his face before he dropped it back to his side. "You see, I don't believe that because Eleanor, she's a sweet girl, you know. She wouldn't have been able to do that to herself. No, she would have needed some help."

"Perhaps she did get help, but it wasn't from me."

"You kill babies, Doc?" Ted asked.

Papa Doc continued to stare at James as he said, "Some babies aren't meant to be born."

"You sick, twisted, motherfucker," James muttered underneath his breath.

All it took was one step forward, and his fist met Papa Doc's face.

Papa Doc fell to the floor. Someone grabbed at his legs and held him down while James sat on his chest.

"You kill babies, huh? Say it again, what you just said."

Blood sputtered from Papa Doc's mouth. He breathed in, and his head went sharply to the right as James punched him.

"Say it again, what you just said!"

"Eleanor," the name escaped from Papa Doc, and James kept his hands by his sides for a moment.

"Huh? What about Eleanor?"

"She...she never came to me. She did it to herself."

"LIAR!" Spit fell from James' mouth as he started to scream. "Where—"

His fist met the side of Papa Doc's face.

"Is—"

Papa Doc heard a crack in the side of his jaw.

"My—"

Someone kicked Papa Doc against his side.

"Child?!"

The words rang in and out of Papa Doc's ears, and then, the pressure on his chest was weightless. He rolled onto his side, and a wave of heat swam up his body and darkened the corners of his vision.

There were two shadows ahead of him. One was holding the other down. They were speaking to each other, but it was gone to the wind before Papa Doc heard it.

Papa Doc closed his eyes.

"Oh God, oh shit. I'm really sorry," A voice near him said, and he felt himself being lifted up.

"Oh, God. Can you hear me?"

Papa Doc blinked his eyes open, and Doug was before him. He barely nodded, and the lights flickered across his vision.

"Okay, okay." He could faintly make out the movement of Doug nodding. "That's good."

Somebody was wailing in the distance. It sounded like a lost puppy out in the freezing winter.

"Oh shit, Huck. Papa Doc, I think he's really dying this time. Can you do something?" Doug said.

It was like a fog had been lifted from Doug's face. Enough so that Papa Doc could stare at him and see the frown lines at the edges of his eyes. Then, the darkness rolled back in, and Papa Doc fell to his knees.

His vision pulsed around him in the tune of his heartbeat. He felt Doug's hands underneath his armpits, trying to lift him back up, but Doug stopped when he saw that Papa Doc had the handsaw in his hand.

Papa Doc lifted himself up. His head tilted forward while he took the handsaw and carved into the last piece of flesh on Huck's leg. The screaming made the waves of ringing return to his ears.

"Hand me," Papa Doc tried to say, but the words only came out as a whisper. Doug moved in closer to hear him. "The poker in the fire."

Doug left his side, and Papa Doc could no longer feel Dave moving underneath his hands. The ringing in his ears became softer. Then, Doug's hand reached for Papa Doc's, placing the metal in his hand. Papa Doc stared at the end of the poker, glowing a faint orange until he saw spots across his vision. He pressed it into Dave's leg.

Thrum, thrum, thrum, the sound echoed around the inside of his skull. Was it screaming, or was there something wrong with his head? It blinded the corners of his vision, and the poker slid through his fingers and landed on the floor. Papa Doc swayed to the side and reached his hand up. He opened his mouth to say something, but someone had put the suture in his hand. In the center of his vision, he saw Doug.

"I can't. He's done for."

"You have to try," Doug said.

Pieces of red pushed their way against the corners of Papa Doc's eyes. Doug's hands were on Papa Doc's back as he moved him to Huck's torso.

His shaking hands gripped the needle and suture as he brought pieces of Dave's skin back together. When he felt himself swaying to another side, Doug grabbed onto his shoulders and repositioned him.

There was no movement. No sign of a shallow breath, only the feeling of warm blood coating Papa Doc's hands.

He put in the last stitch when he stopped seeing red. Doug's arms let go of him, and he fell back onto the floor.

"He's done for," Papa Doc mumbled, but Doug had walked too far away to hear him.

Papa Doc closed his eyes and heard the echoes in the back of his head.

For a while, there was darkness. Until he heard:

Thrum, Thrum, Thrum.

Like the sound of someone knocking on the door.

Silence and darkness.

A howling in the wind.

Was someone screaming? Crying?

A sound, like a lost puppy in a winter storm.

Papa Doc's fingers curled into one another, and it still felt like someone was holding him down.

His mind went to a place where nothing existed, and he stayed there for as long as dreams last.

There was pressure on Papa Doc's chest. He opened his eyes, and his vision was covered in black spots.

"Thank you, thank you," someone said near him. A woman?

The pressure was relieved from his chest, and he blinked away the spots until he could see clearly.

She wiped her eyes while sitting beside him.

"Oh, God, thank you for bringing Huck back to me."

Papa Doc tried to say, "he was done for," but the words never left his lips. Everything in his throat burned. He tried to swallow, but the action brought tears to his eyes.

"Oh, you must be so thirsty and hungry. You've been out for hours. Here, let me get you something."

Papa Doc attempted to reach his arm to point at the kitchen, where his liquor bottle would be, but his hand was shaking so much that he dropped his arm back to his side.

She went to the kitchen anyway and brought him back a glass of clear liquid.

He reached up for the glass, but he could only grab onto the edge before he spilled it all over himself.

"That's okay," she said. "I'll get you another one." She picked up the glass that had fallen onto the floor.

When she came back, she held the glass up to his lips. The smell did not burn his nostrils. He drank from it, and he almost spit it out. It was only water, but he leaned back and drank it until he finished.

"You probably need some food. Let me get you something."

"Who are you?"

She looked at him with her lips pursed together. It was the same expression his mom made whenever she caught him lying to her.

"I'm Huck's wife," she said. "I want to thank you for saving him."

Papa Doc sort of laughed to himself. "Huck couldn't have made it."

"But he did," she said. "Doug told me about how you helped him. I want to thank you."

A knocking reverberated through the whole house, and Papa Doc turned his head to the door.

"I think that you should get that," she said. Without turning back to look at her, he got up to do so. A burning sensation pierced through his shoulder, and he grabbed onto it. With his other hand, he opened the door.

On the other side of the door stood James.

He had a cap in his hand crumbled up into a fist. When he

looked up, his gaze fell immediately to the floor without Papa Doc being able to look at his expression.

"Umm, okay," James started and then sighed. "I came here to apologize. For the fight and for leaving you after you tried to save Huck. I'm sorry."

Papa Doc crossed his arms over his chest.

"I'm a big enough man to hold myself accountable when I've done something wrong, so here I am."

Papa Doc nodded. "Okay, I want you to listen to me now, though. Eleanor never came to me, and that is the honest truth."

"Yes, I know that now. We talked about it. She did it to herself. She wouldn't tell me how. I'm not sure if I want to know. When she told me, I didn't do to her what I did to you, but I...well, we haven't talked in a while." James looked up to the sky. His eyes were glistening. "I wanted to be so upset with her, but I can't. I can't blame her. I've known her all my life. I remember how her father used to take out his belt anytime she so much as walked too far away from the house without his permission. One time, the beatings were so bad that she couldn't even get out of bed. She stayed home a week from school. If he had found out she was pregnant; he would have..." James trailed off.

"So, what're you going to do?"

James stared directly at Papa Doc before he sighed once more. "That's just the thing. I don't know. I would like to leave Thurmond. Find work somewhere, and see parts of this country I've never seen before, but I can't leave Eleanor until after she leaves her father's house. I didn't want to leave here and then come back in a few years and learn that she was still living with him. Back when we were still talking, she mentioned that she would try to stay with her aunt in Kentucky after we graduated. I hope that she's still planning on doing that, and if so, I'll probably leave the same time she does. I really need to get out of this place."

"Well, for your sake, I hope you do. But, before you do leave, I want you to know about those three fetuses in those jars you saw."

"I don't know—"

"They're old. If they had lived, they would have been older than you, but the ones who were going to have them were children themselves. Young girls who didn't have a clue as to what had happened to them, only that it was wrong. They had horrible lives, and what happened to them should have never been done. They were brought to me, and I knew that I was their only chance at not making their lives worse. Some babies are not meant to be born."

"Well, Papa Doc, I trust you did the right thing, but I wanted to tell you something before I go. You're invited to Huck's funeral."

Papa Doc tasted blood in his mouth as he bit down on his tongue.

"I know that you could have probably saved him if I hadn't started the fight. You did try to save him, and I thank you for that, but I don't think there was any way you could have saved him. He was gone from the time he stepped onto those train tracks."

"Huck's gone?" The question came out as nothing more than a whisper.

"Yes. His funeral is tomorrow. The good Lord only knows what will happen to his daughter. Bless her heart. I think she has some family up in-"

"But his wife was just here. She might still be here."

Papa Doc watched as James' expression stretched into disbelief. "Papa Doc, I know you don't spend much time in town, so you probably wouldn't know, but Huck's wife has been gone for a long time. She died like her husband, walking onto those train tracks, but she didn't have anybody try to save her. She was already dead by the time anyone had found her. Look, Papa Doc, I'm really sorry if I hit your head too hard. I think you better take it easy until you heal, okay?"

Papa Doc nodded and slowly closed the door.

THANK GOD

The few people in church that day were nothing more than outlines occupying the empty spaces around the pews. Some were crouched down, and the faint mumblings of their prayers were lost to the wind. Others stared forward as if the priest would walk out at any moment and deliver a sermon.

But the church itself spoke louder than any of the people inside of it could. The lancet windows with colored glass painted the floor in a myriad of orange, red, green, and blue reflections. The spires from the interior ceiling came down to make the floor seem like the sky.

As I sat down, I placed my camera in my lap. I wanted to clasp my hands together, kneel down, and confess everything I had never felt guilty for. The beautiful church effect. I smiled as I remembered Dave's face.

That's a bullshit theory, he had said to me. *You don't feel overwhelmed to confess because beautiful things surround you.*

Yes, you do, I said, but he always skipped over the pages on gothic architecture. Instead of studying, he drew designs for buildings that had no emotion.

"You're a new face around here, aren't you?"

A woman was standing at the end of my aisle. She had a broad smile, and damp red, curly hair clung to her face.

"Yes," I said. I'm staying for a week or so before moving on."

"Well, mind if I sit?"

I shook my head, and she took a spot next to me.

"Tourists are definitely not uncommon here, but they usually come during Mass. They want the big show and all of that. Do you have family here?"

"No, I'm working on a project. I make documentaries about small towns in North America."

"Oh, well," she said and rubbed her hands against her thighs as she sat up straighter to face me. "That's nice. I don't think you'll see much of the town in this church, though." Her laughter echoed around us, and it made me smile.

"That's too bad. Good thing I have an appreciation for architecture."

"Is that right?"

I nodded. "I majored in architecture in college. I liked it, but it was a safety net. I wanted to make movies."

She breathed out a sort of *huh*. "So, are you just filming the towns to show people what it's like here?"

"You could say that. I grew up in a small town and spent my whole time there trying to figure out ways to get out. I thought that all small towns were empty places that became more hollow as the years passed."

"Well, I don't know what town you grew up in, but I hope your films have changed your mindset a bit."

I nodded. "I started making these documentaries after my sister moved to a small town. When she first made the move, I just could not understand why she had wanted to live there, but then I went to visit her. It's a beautiful town with good people in it."

She shook her head and leaned back. "I bet it is. You can never judge a book by its cover. You always need to find what lies underneath the surface."

I agreed and asked her, "Have you lived here for long?"

She sighed. "Well, I lived in Brownsville all of my life before I got married. Then after I got married, I've been in Harper's Ferry since. Been married twenty-three years. Every day I wake up and thank the good Lord for letting me live in this town. I know everyone here, and they're all good people. I could introduce you to some of them, if you like, for your documentary."

"That would be great, thank you," I said. She nodded as if to say *it was no problem*. "Would you like to be in the documentary as well?"

She burst into laughter, and a person sitting in front of us turned to look back.

"Sure, if you'll have me," she said.

"Great. Is an interview okay? I'll just ask you some questions about the town."

"That's fine."

"What time works for you?"

She smiled at that. "There's no time better than the present."

"Right now?"

She nodded.

We sat on the top of a mountain behind the church. The green hills, with their full summer leaves, surrounded us. As she sat down, I set up my camera and turned it on.

"Oh, wait. I'm sorry; I never got your name."

She smiled and raised her head. "That's right. I never told you, and you never told me yours. I'm Elizabeth, but everyone calls me Lizzie."

"Peyton."

She crossed her legs over one another and situated herself on the grass.

I checked the camera once more before saying, "Okay, and we're ready. I am speaking with Elizabeth, a long-time resident of Harper's Ferry. Elizabeth, what is it like to live in Harper's Ferry?"

She leaned back at my question and stared up at the sky. "Well, it's the only place I feel like I could live. It wasn't always like that, of course, but now it is. I feel like I belong here. God has a purpose for everyone, and I do believe that my purpose is to be here."

"Why's that?"

"Oh, well, I don't think anybody can know their true purpose in life unless God spells it out for them in the clouds. It's more of a feeling. When I think about moving away from this place, I feel sick. It's like I'm about to throw up, but I just can't do it yet," she said and laughed. Then she sighed. "I guess it's also that I feel at peace here. I grew up outside Harper's Ferry, as I told you earlier. I lived in the mountains in just about the middle of nowhere. That's what it felt like, at least. I loved going on walks by myself and being alone up there. I couldn't imagine living in a place where I would take ten steps outside of my house and see my neighbors. Here I am, though, and I love being here. I really do. I also love everyone here. Love thy neighbors. I took that bit of teaching from the Bible to heart. I really do think that this world would be a better place if a lot more people did that. Everyone deserves to be loved."

"That's really sweet. I haven't mentioned this to the viewers yet, but Elizabeth and I met at St. Peter's Catholic Church. Would you say that your religious beliefs connect you more to this place?"

"That's difficult to answer," she said and started laughing again. It was short, though, before she said, "Yes and no, I guess. I've been religious all my life, and I didn't feel this divine awakening when I started living in Harper's Ferry. But, after the first mass I attended in St. Peter's Catholic Church, I heard this little voice inside my head. It said, 'Thank God you're finally saved.' When I tell most people that story, they get freaked out. But it wasn't anything scary. If anything, it made me calmer. It was nothing more than a thought, like when you get a song stuck in your head. Ever since then, I've been going to that church. I grew up Baptist and became Catholic to stay at St. Peter's. Baptist, Catholic, Christian, it doesn't make a bit of difference to me. We all have different ideas of God, and so my God is not your God, not his God, not her God, but we all know that we can care for those around us like He cares for us."

"That's an interesting statement. Would you like to elaborate more on that?"

"Oh, well, I guess so, if there's going to be people watching this."

"Let's hope so," I said, and she smiled.

"Okay then. I've seen too many people think that God is black and white and if you break any of His rules, you're done for. I guess some people might feel the Holy Presence when they tell others how to behave, but I couldn't imagine how. Even then, when they tell others how to act, they are forgetting that they should not judge, or they too will be judged. Some people need to pick up their Bible more than pointing a finger at someone. You can't just pick out parts of the Bible that you want to focus on and forget the most important message."

"And what's that?"

"Well, I feel God the most when I love and accept those around me, so I think that love and acceptance are the two most important messages. There's no way we can know what anybody's going through. Loving and accepting them will help them more than judging ever will. Don't get me wrong, if someone needs help, then by all means, get them help. But help should not be judgment; it should come from deep in a person's heart. This is something that more people need to keep in their minds: At the end of the day, we're all God's people, and we're all just trying to do our best."

"That's a really beautiful message. I actually grew up Baptist as well."

"Oh, and are you still?"

"No. I don't think that I'm anything right now. I believe in some ideas found in religion, like fate, and that everything was created for a reason. But I think that it's more complicated than any of us could understand. I guess I'm sort of a spiritual person in that way, but I haven't found a religion that has values that I completely agree with."

"You probably won't find one," she said. "You choose one that you are drawn to, and you spread its message of love and kindness."

I shook my head and stared at the ground before looking back at her. "I wish there was someone like you at my church growing up."

"There probably was. You just probably didn't know her."

"I doubt it. It was a tiny church, and everyone had, what did you say? Ah, black and white thinking."

She shrugged. "Even in small churches, I guarantee you that there's one person who thinks differently. Life has a way of surprising you, you know."

My chest felt hollow, and I bit down on my tongue before saying, "Yeah, um," I stumbled and looked back at the camera. My battery was approaching the halfway line. "We went a bit off topic."

"If you see me more while you're here, you'll find that that's a common occurrence."

I laughed. "Back on the topic of Harper's Ferry, though. What people, places, and things do you like the most about this place?"

"Well, with that question, there's a lot that I have to say, but I'm going to keep it short. I love the locals, but I also love meeting the tourists. Everyone has such a different perspective on life. It's fascinating to hear about all of them. There's no one place in the town that I prefer over another. I love all of it, and I wouldn't know how to tell you how great this place is unless you see it for yourself. So, come, see it for yourself," she said and started laughing again. "As for the things, there's always something to do. I work with the church and set up activities there, but I also work in the community. There's always some sort of event going on."

"Okay. This is really great. Thank you, Elizabeth, for having this interview with me. I think that's all that I need."

"Thank you, yourself," she said as I started to put the camera away. "I felt like we had a good conversation."

I only nodded.

"Now, tell me, how many people are going to be watching this documentary?"

I didn't look up at her, instead, I continued to try to put my camera in its bag as I shrugged and said, "I always hope that it's going to be a lot, but the numbers never add up to what I'm expecting."

"Well, every person counts," she said, and I looked back at her.

"You know, I think that I was meant to meet you today."

She crinkled her eyes and held her head back before saying, "Of course you were. Everything happens for a reason."

I only smiled and shook my head, and as I got up, she did too. I held out my hand to shake hers, but she pulled me into a hug. My arms hung limply at my sides, shocked that she had decided to hug me. *When was the last time someone had done that? I* thought before my arms slowly reached up to hug her back. The whole time, I hoped my camera bag wouldn't fall off my shoulder and hit her.

As she pulled away from me, she said, "Now, don't make yourself a stranger while you're here." She patted me on the shoulder.

I was about twenty minutes from the hillside motel as the sky settled into a clear, cold blue around me. The radio played a song that sounded like every other song it had played that day.

I finished the last of my cheeseburger, one hand still on the steering wheel, as I tossed the wrapper onto the floor to join the others. My phone buzzed in the seat next to me, and the call came through my car. I accepted it.

My sister answered, drawing out the letters in "hey" like she always did when she was tired.

"Hey."

"What town are you in today?"

I turned down a corner on the road. "Harper's Ferry, West Virginia. I'll probably be here until the end of the week."

"And where will you be going then?"

I shook my head, even though she couldn't see me. It was more out of instinct. "The adventure is in the unknown," I responded.

"Okay, well, just keep me updated with where you are."

"I'll try, but no guarantees. How's everything up there?"

"Oh, you know, the same."

I leaned back when she said that. She would usually tell me that it wasn't safe for me to not update her.

"Betsey and I found a new hiking trail with the most spectacular views," she continued.

"Ah, the quiet life of a married couple."

"Yeah. We should all go on the trail the next time you're up here. You know, our small town is still open for your documentary."

"I know, and it's on my list."

"Well, if you can push it closer to the top of your list, Mom and Dad are visiting next weekend, and they would really like to see you. They miss you a lot."

My tongue pressed against the roof of my mouth. My fingers started to ache from how tightly I clutched the steering wheel. "Next weekend's too close for me to drive to the other side of the country," I mumbled.

"Sure, Mr. Drove-from-a-town-outside-of-Montreal-to-Florida-in-three-days."

"It was four days."

"Sure, but it's okay. I'll tell them that you had a project come up."

"Okay," I said. "Love you."

"I love you too, and I miss you."

"Bye."

"Bye."

~

I stared at my phone as I walked across the parking lot to my motel. I had three missed calls. One from my mom and two from my dad. Tears were building up in the corners of my eyes. I shook my head and played the first message from my mom.

"Hey, um, this is me, your mom. I know we haven't spoken in such a long time, but I really, well, I just really miss you, and I'm sorry. I know that word's not enough, but I am more sorry than you'll ever know. Your sister and you—"

I deleted the message, and my thumb faltered over the message from my dad. The screen was nothing more than a white blur when I finally pressed down on it. My phone fell and clattered to the ground as my hands and knees met the steps.

"Please, help me," a man mumbled near me. I turned to the sound. My ears were ringing.

He was sitting on the stairs. The entrance doors were only steps away from him.

"Take me inside, please," he said, and blood sputtered out from his mouth and painted down the sides of his face. He had one leg stretched out in front of him, and the other, I thought, was bent to him. But, when I looked down, the other leg was nothing more than torn pieces of flesh ending just below his pelvis. Blood poured from his wound and stained the concrete steps.

"Please, I need to be saved."

"Help!" I screamed. "This man needs help!"

"Take me inside."

"I can't!" I said.

"Please."

"Help! I need a doctor!"

He started breathing heavily. It almost sounded sort of like crying. "Please, just take me inside the church."

"What?"

He reached out for me, but I felt his touch at the back of my shoulder.

"Hey, you alright?"

I turned to face the voice behind me. It was a young woman with cropped blond hair. Smoke trailed from the cigarette that dangled between her fingers.

"This man needs help," I said and looked back at the man I was pointing at. On those steps, there was no one. The blood stains were cleaned as if they had never been there.

"I don't know what you're on, but I think you should probably get some sleep."

"I-I'm not on anything," I stuttered, and I couldn't stop staring at the spot. "He was just here."

"Did you need me to call someone for you?"

My gaze faltered slightly past the spot to my phone. The ringing in my ears had stopped.

"Hello? Hello? Is everything okay?" A voice came out of the phone.

I reached for it. The screen was cracked, but I could still see that the call had been happening for five minutes. It was my dad.

"Son? Is everything okay? Please, tell me. I don't even know where you are," I heard him say quietly to himself. "Where are you?"

I hung up the call and put my phone into my back pocket as I started to stand up.

"Are you sure you don't need anything?" The girl asked. Her voice trailed off as I walked further away.

"Yeah, I'm fine. I'm just going to get some sleep," I said. My voice sounded strange in my ears like I was listening to a recording of myself talking.

"Okay then," she dragged out the words.

Did she really not see him? Am I going crazy? My phone started buzzing in my pocket. I grabbed it and saw that it was my Dad trying to call again. *How did they even get my number?*

I pressed my thumb against the power button and shut it

down. When it was back in my pocket, I looked over my shoulder. Only the girl was leaning against the post by the empty stairs.

He had wanted to go inside. He was so close to the door. What had happened? I held my head in my hands. *What is wrong with me?*

I usually turned off all the lights to sleep, but I kept the lamp and the TV on. *For tonight, at least,* I thought. My phone was in my camera bag now. It would stay there for the rest of the night.

One, two, three, four, I started to count. *Why was he there? Five, six, seven, eight.*

My body was heavy in bed. I needed to get up to go to the bathroom, but I wouldn't move. *Nine, ten, eleven, twelve. What is wrong with me? Thirteen, fourteen, fifteen.* I closed my eyes, only to open them back up when I reached twenty and close them again. *Stop thinking. Just go to sleep.*

The last number I remember reaching was 374. If I dreamt of anything at all that night, I didn't remember it.

The coffee cup burned against the palm of my hand, but I didn't put it down. I could have sat on one of the benches and put it on the floor, but walking felt good. A faint ache pulsed in the back of my head, but the coffee would help it to go away once it cooled down. With my other hand, I pressed the bridge of my nose and closed my eyes. *I need to go to sleep.*

"Fuck. What is wrong with me?" When I opened my eyes, I was standing in front of the steps leading up to the church. "Fuck. How did you get here?" I said. *My bad. I hope you won't hold that against me.* I smiled and wanted to laugh, but the sound remained, choked at the back of my throat. Someone slapped me on the shoulder. I jolted forward, and a bit of my coffee spilled onto the steps.

"You're becoming a daily visitor to this church, like me," Elizabeth's voice echoed in my ears. I should have looked down, but I looked directly at her. She took a step back when she saw my face. I don't think she meant to, but I turned my head back to the ground.

And then, she started laughing. "Well, you look like death himself this morning. Now tell me, honey, what's on your mind?" She leaned closer to me and whispered, "Are you in trouble?"

I shook my head, and she moved away. This time, when I looked at her, she wasn't smiling.

"I didn't sleep well last night, that's all. I thought I did, but I woke up this morning, and I guess I didn't."

Her staring at me made the ache in my head tighten like a string, and she grabbed onto the ends of it and pulled.

"Say, is that coffee all you've had for breakfast?"

I nodded.

"Well, I was just heading up to the café to get me some breakfast. Would you like to come with me?"

"Sure," I said because I thought that one word would make the ache go away.

We set the food on a table outside, the mountains were behind Elizabeth. Despite her insistence on calling her Lizzie, I still felt the need to call her Elizabeth. It was like referring to a teacher by her first name.

I moved the food around my plate.

"You know, you need to eat something if you're not feeling that great. I don't know what's in this food, but I swear it's the best I've ever had. It will cure whatever is wrong."

I picked up a forkful of my food, put it in my mouth, chewed, and swallowed. I tried not to think about what it tasted like. I was being absurd, I needed to eat. I took larger portions, and continued to chew and swallow.

"That's good," Elizabeth remarked. "You should be eating something if you've been drinking that stuff. I don't know how you even drink it. It makes me so jittery."

"The coffee?"

"Yes. When I drink just one cup of it, I feel like, well, I feel like I could run a marathon." She covered her mouth when she started laughing and leaned closer to me. "Now, I'm the type of person that I only run if something's chasing me."

A smile formed across my lips, but I couldn't make myself laugh with her. "I'm not much of a coffee drinker myself," I said.

She leaned back and nodded in understanding. "Tell me, what's going on?"

I shrugged. "It's nothing, really. Just a lot of things happening all at once again. I think everything will be better tomorrow, after I get some sleep tonight."

"I know what you mean. Sometimes so many things press into the mind that they start to seem like they're meaningless, but they're not. They're still pressing away until you feel like you're going insane."

"Yeah, that's a lot like it, actually."

"I understand if you don't want to talk about what you're going through right now. Sometimes, it's better to deal with things on your own, but I have all morning to sit here and listen if you feel you need to get rid of whatever's pressing on you."

I nodded. Tears burned in the corners of my eyes, but I blinked them away. "I, um, it's just a lot of things. My sister called yesterday. She wanted me to come to her house - she lives in Oregon - because my parents are visiting her next week. And then my parents wouldn't stop calling. I don't even know how they got my number. I tried to listen to a voicemail that my dad left when I tripped over something. I thought I saw something, but it wasn't actually there, and the phone, or maybe I, accidentally called my dad. And now he and my mom won't stop calling, and I turned my phone off because all I could hear was ringing and the man's voice saying that he wanted to go into the church."

"St. Peter's Church?"

"Maybe." A tear fell down my face, and I put my head in my hands.

"Aw, honey, it's okay. Just let it out."

"You know what, I'm sorry. This is stupid. I should go back to the motel and get some sleep."

"No, it's not," Elizabeth said. "Who was this man that wanted to go into the church?"

"I don't think that he was actually there. He seemed so real, though, but there was a girl right near him that asked me what was wrong. I don't think that she saw him."

"Well, then, there's not much that I can tell you other than that you might want to see a shrink."

"I know," I said and wiped my eyes with the backs of my hands.

"You don't have to tell me if you don't want to, but what's this whole thing going on with your family?"

I sighed and continued to stare down at the table. I felt so immature, but I didn't want to look at her.

"There wasn't anything going on for the longest time until last night. I haven't spoken to my parents since I was in college. They'll call occasionally, and last night wasn't the first time my sister asked if I wanted to come to her house and meet my parents there. My sister is so much stronger than I'll ever be. My parents asked for her forgiveness, and she gave it to them."

"Forgiveness for what?"

"For kicking her out; for not accepting her. My parents figured out that she was gay when she was fourteen. She was still a child, and they kicked her out of the house because they lived by the Bible, which was black and white to them. There was no room for gray area. The next thing I knew, she was on my doorstep. She and I both got extra jobs, and we worked our asses off to afford an apartment to live in while she finished high school, and I finished college. I will do anything and everything for my sister. She deserved to have a normal childhood. She deserved to be loved by my parents, but they abandoned her. When my sister was standing on my doorstep, I promised myself I would never forgive them."

"You can't make a promise that lasts forever."

I nodded. "I know, I know, and she knew that. She was the one who they kicked out, and she forgave them. They have lunch with her and her wife nearly every month. From what I can tell, everything's fine now. They're accepting and supportive, but it seems too late for me. I mean, at what point do you go past the point of no return? I know that I should see them and try to forgive them, but I don't know what to say or do. I don't know if I can still forgive them because, when I see their faces, I just know that I'll see my sister standing on that doorstep again."

"I'm sorry," Elizabeth said. I looked up at her, even though I knew my eyes were red and puffy. The corners of her eyes and mouth were wrinkled.

"I'm sorry that happened to you and your sister. I don't believe that God works through hate and judgment, but rather through kindness and forgiveness. God worked through your parents when they accepted your sister, and she forgave them, and I really think that you should call your parents and maybe even visit them whenever you go back to your sister's house if you feel ready. Now, I've never been in your situation, but I have had to forgive many good people as well as myself a few times before. From my experiences, I can tell you that I've never been able to fully move on until I forgave. You do what you think is right, but at the end of the day, don't put yourself farther back in life than you need to be."

I nodded. I wanted to tell her thank you, but my throat

constricted to form a lump. She grabbed my hand, and I let her take it.

"Now, I think that you need some time alone to make that phone call or even just to process this. If you need to talk again, I'll be at the church for most of the afternoon."

I stared at the table as I felt her hand slip through mine. Her footsteps were lost among the people walking out of the café.

Alone, I stared out at the West Virginia hills. Birds whistled their songs through the sky, and the wind brought chills up my arms. I barely held onto my phone while I traced the crack along its screen. It could slip through my hand and fall onto the grass, and maybe another crack would form against it, and maybe it wouldn't.

I could always tell them that I had fallen and that my phone was broken and I couldn't get a new one anytime soon. And then, I realized just how funny that phrase was: *I could always tell them.* I hadn't told them anything in years. Mom, Dad – if I saw them in person, would they even know it was me?

I saw them sitting with my sister and her wife. What did they talk about? The weather? That made me laugh.

I pressed my sister's contact. Three rings and she picked up.

"Hey, how are you doing? Dad called me yesterday. He said that you answered one of his calls and that things sounded weird."

"Yeah, I'm okay," I said. "I'm not hurt or anything. I guess I just fell."

"You guess?"

I pressed the bridge of my nose, closed my eyes, and took a deep breath.

"Why did you forgive Mom and Dad?"

I heard her let out a breath on the other end. "Is that why you won't come here?"

"Could you just tell me why?" The question came out as

nothing more than a whisper as the inside of my throat began to burn.

"Okay, yeah," she said, and her voice was slowly straining like she was trying to convince herself that she could do this. "For a really long time, I didn't think that I could ever forgive them. Even after I started talking to them on the phone for a while, up to the point that we decided to meet in person. I chose a public place to meet – a coffee shop – and I had two friends come along with me in case they tried to make me go to conversion therapy or something." There was a moment of silence at the other end. "It was there, when we were finally able to sit down and talk to each other face to face, I realized that everything that we had talked about on the phone - about how they were more sorry than I could ever imagine, how their parents had taught them that they would know God's love by fearing him, and how they learned that - after all the years they spent without us - nobody can find love like that." Another pause at the other end, and the corners of my eyes burned. "They're still not perfect, you know, but they're trying. Did I tell you that they now go to an LGBTQ+ friendly church, and the pastor is gay?"

"Really?"

"Yeah," she said. "And you know, being with them, I've learned that I'm still not perfect either. Sometimes, when they come over for dinner and stuff, everything will be great. We'll be talking about a funny past memory of something, and then those memories come back to me of all the nights that I thought would never end and the days that I thought I would never see, and I'll just feel this heat rise up into my body. It's like I've been out in the sun for hours, and all I want to do is scream at them. It feels like nothing will ever be okay. But Mom usually notices when I tense up. She said that the mood around me shifts. Even after all those years I spent growing up without her, she can still read my every emotion."

"So what do you do then? When you feel like that?"

"We talk about it – the past and the memories that don't make us laugh. We've had many awkward dinners, a lot more than peaceful ones. But, you know what? Even after all of it, I'm glad we're working through it. I know that every person with family problems has their own story, but I think that if I had never gone to that coffee shop with them, I would have lived with a weight on my chest for the rest of my life. Every single conversation we've had since I've started connecting with them again has lifted a fraction of that weight. I've learned something from all of it too. You can only save yourself from hurting so many times. Eventually, you have to let someone help you."

The tears were warm against my face as they fell from the corners of my eyes. My breath was heavy, and shuddered against my whole body.

"Are you still there?"

"Yeah," I said, and the word broke apart in my mouth. "I think that I need help."

She sighed in understanding. "Are you coming to Oregon next week to get it?"

"Yes," and the confirmation made the muscles in my chest tighten around my heart.

"It'll be nice to see you again," she said. Even though she couldn't see me, I nodded. "Oregon's a lot further away for you than my coffee shop was, but I think it will be a journey worth taking."

"Thank you," I said.

"Goodbye."

I hung up the phone.

I could see candlelight flickering against the church's walls from the windows outside. Tears slid down my face and neck. I didn't wipe them away. Nobody was outside to see me, to stare at the person who was crying, except for Elizabeth. She was standing on the front steps of the church like she knew I would be coming there.

When she held out her arms for me, I fell into them like I had so many times with my mom while I was a child.

"It's okay," she murmured. "Are you fixing things with your parents?"

I nodded against her shoulder.

"Well, thank God, then," she said. "You're finally saved."

~1~

Our house wasn't at the end of the road, but it was the last house on the road. The only people who came to this part of the street were the ones who wanted to turn around, and most people turned around in a neighbor's driveway before they came here. As I walked, I wrapped my cardigan around myself and tucked my hands into my armpits. It had been an unusually warm winter in Point Pleasant, but the cold air still bit at my exposed hands and the sides of my face.

A deer peered at me from between two trees. Its beady eyes glinted in the rising sun. When it heard my feet crunching against the gravel, it stopped.

"It's okay," I said to it. My dad used to tell me that deer think they're invisible when they stand still. I waved at it, and its ears twitched in response. I walked away from it, toward the end of the street. To the piles of rubble. I picked up the pieces of gravel like a child learning how to play with toy blocks. The rocks created soft dents across my palms.

I could build a city out of these blocks, I thought. *One by one, I could stack them all up and make a whole town for myself.*

There must be less than a hundred blocks and some gravel, not enough to build anything. I heard the school bus driving down the hill, and I dropped the rocks I was holding and ran back to where I had come from.

~2~

It was the start of the New Year, 1968, and people were still on edge after the Silver Bridge Disaster. Forty-six people died crossing that bridge, bringing home Christmas presents to their families when it collapsed.

Those who lived mourned in their own ways.

After the tragedy, kids at school became obsessed with the Mothman. Some people thought they saw him before the bridge collapsed. The stoners got high and believed they connected with him in another dimension. The Christians and Catholics thought that he was the devil. Guys claimed they met the Mothman in their backyards and fought him off to impress girls. Girls declared that it was nothing more than a mutated bird from all of the nearby radiation. They were only trying to ward off the guys' attention. It all made me want to scream. Whenever I heard someone utter the word "Mothman," or "red eyes," or even just "wings," I walked away, picking at the skin around my nails and on my lips.

They're all such assholes, I would think to myself.

A week after the tragedy, when rumors about the Mothman started, Billy had said he had fought the Mothman off the football field during Mrs. Johnson's class. The room was silent as Mrs. Johnson dropped the piece of chalk she was holding. It clattered and then snapped on the floor.

I wanted to go up and hug her and yell at Billy for being such an asshole and a shitty person. Mrs. Johnson's husband had been one of those who had died on that bridge, and if Billy didn't know that, then he was an even shittier person for not knowing it. I pinched my wrist to distract myself and tried to wipe away the tears before anyone could see them. Tears fell from my face as my heart began to race.

She brought her hands up to her face, masking the sobs that brought chills across my arms. Her whole body shook.

"Class dismissed," she said before turning her face to the ground and walking back to her desk. Mrs. Johnson took a deep breath and dropped her hands. Her face was a bruised red color, and her eyes were bloodshot. Most students remained sitting, shell-shocked, so it wasn't hard for me to push my way out of the room.

I ran to the bathroom.

In the safety of a stall, I locked the door and cried.

~3~

The first time I heard the shadows was that night.

One step after the other on the stairs. The footsteps echoed and grew louder until they reverberated against the walls. An animal could've made such a sound—footsteps and then silence.

But an animal wouldn't have been able to turn the doorknob on my bedroom door.

Something fought against the locked door, turning the knob back and forth and back and forth and back and forth. It sounded like wind chimes outside during a thunderstorm. I lay still in my bed and closed my eyes as tightly as possible. Like a child, I believed that if I couldn't see it, it wasn't real.

It's only in your mind, I thought. *The stuff the kids are saying at school is getting to you.* Silence filled the spaces between each turn of the knob. It's not real. I repeated to myself until I fell into a dreamless sleep.

The mourning dove's cries woke me in the morning. I got up from bed, stretched, and looked out the window. The street outside was desolate, and a gentle wind tickled the few remaining leaves on the trees. The warm sunlight pouring in through the windowpanes spread across my face.

January skies were usually gray, so I closed my eyes and basked in the sunlight. When I felt settled, I walked over to my bedroom door. A bundle of lavender from last season's plants, held together by twine, hung from my doorknob. I brought it up to my nose and inhaled deeply, taking the scent in and exhaling. I opened the door and stepped out of the attic, my bedroom. I heard every floorboard creak when I walked down the stairs. Standing still, I swore I could hear my own heartbeat. I walked down the staircase quickly, shutting my bedroom door behind me.

When the pads of my feet landed on the wooden floor, I

opened the door at the bottom of the stairway. I listened for Mom and Dad walking around and heard the sounds of cabinets shutting in the kitchen. I turned the corner towards the kitchen, but my gaze caught on a streak of light across the floor. I followed it up to see my grandmother's old room; the door cracked open.

On the doorframe, I looked at the ink lines scattered across it. Some of them covered each other to where they were indistinguishable, but I knew most of them from memory.

Theo – 4, Evelyn -3, William – 6, Theo – 9, Evelyn – 8, and then the one that I'm named after, my dad's sister, Allison – 7.

The names continued, filling up the whole door frame, and all of them were on my dad's side of the family. The lines marked their heights. I suppose they are my mom's family, too, since this house became a part of her blood when she married my dad.

"Allison, Alissa," the names turned over on my tongue, and with them, I remembered the last time I saw my aunt.

It was the summer before high school. Nana was still alive back then, but everyone knew she was living on borrowed time and couldn't travel, so we had the family reunion in the backyard. My mom spent weeks braiding flower crowns for my cousins, cooking all the recipes Nana had written and kept in the tin beside the oven, and washing everything she could wash in the house. The house smelled like soap for a week afterward. A laugh escaped from my lips.

Allison had her hair pulled up in a ponytail and wore the ruffled cream shirt Nana had gotten her for Christmas a couple of years back. It was baggy and looked absolutely awful on her, but she didn't seem to mind. Was her hair brown? I thought it was, but in the last letter she wrote me, she told me she had dyed it red. That was all I could think of her having now.

Does her hair lighten in the sun down there in Florida like my dishwater blonde hair does here in July? I imagined her hair turning a light orange and saying it was in fashion while bouncing it. That made me laugh again. Then, Nana's face came into my mind, but it wasn't the face I saw at the reunion. No, it was the face she had two days before she died. Her mouth, missing most of its teeth, hung open in an O. Her hair looked like dandelion fuzz across her pillow, and her skin clung to her bones like a wet bathing suit. Her breaths came out shallow and ragged. With its embroidered images of lavender, the quilt seemed to swallow her whole.

Standing in the doorway, I saw that the quilt remained tucked into the mattress. Mom had framed the pillowcase Nana had loved so dearly those last few days – the one her mother had embroidered the Lord's Prayer onto – and hung it on the wall above the nightstand.

It was the same pillow we had found the clump of feathers tangled together to resemble a halo underneath it. When Mom saw it while cleaning after Nana passed, she gasped.

"What is it?" I asked her. When my gaze trailed from the crown to her eyes, I saw that she was crying.

"It's a Death Crown," she said. "I've never seen one before, but my mom told me about them. She said one of them was under your great grandma's pillow when she passed."

"But what is it?" I asked.

Mom wiped away her tears and said, "Oh, there's a lot of theories on them. Some of them good, some of them bad. I like to stick with the good ones, though, and the good ones say that if you find this under a loved one's pillow after they pass, that means they've made it to heaven."

I wiped away one of my own tears that had fallen. I shut the bedroom door behind me and walked into the kitchen. I opened my mouth to say good morning, but the kitchen was empty. I walked around, going into the dining room and peering into the living room beside it, but no one was home.

It's an old house, and old houses make noise, I told myself, and the thought settled me a bit as I filled the kettle with water and set it to boil.

When the steam circled across the mug, I held the cup of tea in my hands and stared out the window. A squirrel was running across the backyard, no doubt confused about the warm weather. It sniffed at the holes in the ground that we had covered to preserve them for our plants come spring and summer. Occasionally, I would look down and watch the lemon slices swirl around the transparent green liquid. I brought it to my lips, sipped, and watched the sky lighten.

I thought I should go out today, and as I did so, I tried to rationalize spending money on gas. *I can get a part-time job somewhere;* I came up with my usual response. *Besides, wasting a beautiful day like today would be so sad.*

After my last sip, I got up from the table, placed my cup in the sink, and walked back up to the attic to change.

~4~

I walked across the grass to the curb and got into my slug bug. I turned it on and checked the gas—less than half a tank.

Go to the gas station. You need gas anyways, I thought.

"Two things that don't grow on trees are gas and money," Dad loved to say. Gas was one of the first things to go when the coal mine laid him off, and he had to resort to digging six-foot deep holes for a paycheck. "And buses don't make you pay for gas, so you better be taking the buses," he said. But it was Saturday, and the only buses that ran to the end of Whispering Way were school buses.

I put my foot on the pedal and started driving.

There wasn't anybody outside on Whispering Way. Still, the remnants of them having enjoyed the strange, warmer weather earlier showed as I saw lawn chairs, beer bottles, and basketballs strewn across driveways from the corner of my eye. I turned the corner and let the hum of the tires crunching across the road fill my mind.

~5~

There were a couple of kids from school at the gas station. I had definitely seen them at school, but I couldn't remember their names for the life of me. They sat on the hood of a Mustang that they had all, no doubt, arrived here in. Some of them were drinking Cokes and passing around bits of food, while a couple of them were curled up and brushing their fingers through each other's hair and drawing circles on their arms.

It's nine in the morning, I thought. *Calm the fuck down.*

But, as I opened the door, I wondered how it would feel for someone to brush his fingers through my hair.

My thoughts left me when I saw the magazine rack as soon as I walked into the store. There, a lady stared back at me. She only seemed to be a few years older than me, but she had her eyes downcast and her lips slightly parted in a way that I would never be able to do without falling into a fit of laughter. Blue eyeshadow spread across her lids. I picked up the magazine and traced over the eyeshadow.

She's probably traveled everywhere and has seen everything, I thought. *She must've traveled across the whole country by now, been to all fifty states. She's probably bored with the United States now and is trying to move somewhere else.* Where would she go? France? Italy? London?

"Hey girl," a voice said beside me and startled me into gripping the magazine. The person laughed, and I turned to where the sound came from.

Amelia stood beside me. She had her brown hair pulled up into high braids and was wearing a short yellow skirt that my mom would have scoffed at. When Ellen, Amelia's older sister, came home for Christmas Break at the start of December, I went to their house to say "hi" to an old friend. That was all I ever said to them nowadays.

"What'cha got there?" Amelia asked, peering over my shoulder, and I showed her the magazine. For some reason, I expected her to laugh at me like she had after the pimple incident, but instead, her mouth opened in surprise.

"Do you like it?" She asked in a sly voice, and I was the one laughing. "What?!" She asked.

"Of course I do," I said between breaths. "She's stunning."

Amelia shook her head. "No, she's fucking gorgeous." She grabbed my hand, and I was taken back to when I was seven, and she had to hold onto my hand so I wouldn't run away from her in the woods.

Funny how we used to run around our woods, playing hide and seek with one another. I was always "it" because I was the youngest. It didn't seem fair at the time, and it still doesn't. I was always looking for the best hiding place for the one day that I wouldn't be it. My best idea was underneath Jenny's porch, but I dismissed it when she found a snake there the summer before I started junior high. Junior high was when everything changed.

Ellen and Amelia were already in high school when I woke up one morning in seventh grade and saw a red dot with a yellow, inflamed circle in the center of my forehead. I asked Amelia for help. I remembered she had acne that coated her head and cheeks when she was my age, but by the time she had gotten to high school, it had all cleared up. When she saw my problem, she laughed at me.

Now, looking at her, it seems like nothing, but at the time, I felt like I was having one of those nightmares where I showed up to school naked.

She told me that one of her friends gave her birth control pills. *Amelia was taking drugs?* I asked her if her mom knew, and she did. Of course, Jenny did, and of course, she wouldn't have a problem with it. She was a never-married mom with two girls and a self-proclaimed feminist. Many older ladies in Point Pleasant moved to walk on the other side of the street when they saw Jenny coming along, as if they would catch her "radical" beliefs like cooties.

"Where are we going?" I asked. She dragged me until we were directly under one of the few fluorescent lights scattered around the ceiling. The magazine was still clutched in my hand.

She was giggling like a schoolgirl, and a thought came to me.

"Are you high?"

That only made her giggle even more. And then she said, "Of course not. But this is fun, isn't it?"

"Yeah, sure," I remarked, not fully convinced she wasn't high.

Amelia rolled her eyes at me, but she was smiling. "Here, close your eyes," she said.

I felt like I should have hesitated, but Amelia's energy was infectious. I closed my eyes and heard her pull something out of her bag and open a container. Then, I felt a soft pressure against my eyelids.

~6~

The whole drive home, I kept staring at myself in the rearview mirror, my green eyes enhanced by the blue eye shadow. I lowered my eyes and set my mouth agape. Every once in a while, my gaze would falter to my bag, where I kept the blue eye shadow.

"Keep it," Amelia had said, "it looks better on you than it ever did on me."

"Fucking gorgeous," I whispered to myself, and I felt like it. I felt it all the way until I walked into my house.

"Ah, there she is," Dad said as soon as I turned the key in the door and opened it. My heart stopped. I looked at the ground and started trying to walk toward the stairs that led to my room.

"Hi, Dad," I mumbled. *Did he come home early from work?* I thought. *He must have if he's here.*

"No, stop. We need to talk."

I wanted, more than anything, to continue to walk, but I stopped. I did continue to stare at the ground, though, as long as I could.

"Alissa," he said and took a deep sigh. "Listen, I know how kids are these days. You might not think that I do, but I do, and I know that they love to go and hang out with their friends and whatever, but, honey, we don't have enough money to –"

I nodded, keeping my head down, but I felt his gaze burrowing into me.

"Why won't you look at me?"

I didn't have any response to speak of. My heartbeat was in my fingertips.

"What's wrong?"

I felt a sort of relief settle within me. I shrugged, hoping that he would think that I was just being emotional and let me go to my room, but instead, he grabbed onto my shoulders. He brought me closer to him, and I raised my head. When he saw my eyes, his face dropped. I struggled out of his grasp, and he held onto me for a second before letting me go.

"What the—" He started softly. I started walking away before he began yelling. "What the hell is on your face?!"

Tears burned down my cheeks. I rubbed my eyes, and blue eye shadow coated my hands.

"You look like a hooker!" My dad yelled. I climbed up the stairs to the attic. His footsteps trailed after mine, but I ran through my door and slammed it behind me. The wooden panel shook on its rusty hinges, causing the knob to shake as I ensured it was locked.

His heavy steps echoed up the stairs leading to the attic. He turned the doorknob back and forth, and it rattled back and forth and back and forth and back and forth.

I fell to my knees and pushed myself away from its rattling, closer to my bed.

"Take that makeup off!" He yelled through the door. "I won't have a prostitute living in my house!"

He continued to bang at the door and turn the knob, and the sobs rocked through my body. I brought my knees to my chest and wrapped my arms around them. If the knob were to break and it could open...

In the corner of my vision, I only saw red.

I turned, ever so slightly, to face the window. Behind the fragile glass, a shadow lifted its clawed hand and scratched down. I pressed my palms against my ears and shut my eyes away from the creature's glowing, red eyes.

"Go away," I muttered. *This isn't real*, I reminded myself. *The stuff people say at school is getting to you. This isn't real. It's all in your head. How could you be so sensitive? None of it is real.*

I opened my eyes slowly. A car passed by, and when its headlights glinted past my window, I saw an 'X' scratched into the glass. The creature dropped its hand to its side, and two leathery wings shot up. When it beat them against its back, the wind whipped past the house and shook the walls.

One, two, three flaps, and then it was gone.

I gasped for air, my hands pressing into my chest. Dark spots danced across my vision. My gaze faltered from the window to the doorknob, where I saw that it stood still. The sight steadied my shaking limbs, and I crawled into bed. The dark spots never left my vision; they only overtook it as I fell asleep.

~7~

There was the sound of something scraping against the walls of the house. An echo of a bang and then footsteps stumbling across the floor. A pressure pushed against my eyes, and I had to force them open to see the sunlight glinting off the blue eye shadow on my hands. I sat up in my bed and looked towards the window.

It was already morning.

I let out a sigh and curled up into a ball, pressing the palms of my hands against my eyes. My stomach rumbled. *When was the last time I ate?* I thought, followed by, *When was the last time I took of the plants?*

Certainly not yesterday, but had I taken care of them the day before? If they fail, too, Dad will be even more upset. One of the only good things I have going for me is taking care of those little plants.

I got out of bed, grabbed my coat, put on my shoes, and walked downstairs.

The first stop was the bathroom. I scrubbed my hands and face raw until I could no longer see any traces of blue.

I attempted to make it to the basement, where the babies were no doubt struggling to survive without my help, my heart stopped as I saw a shadow create an elongated line across the wall.

"Good morning," Mom said, appearing from around the corner. I opened my mouth, but it took me a minute before the words fell out.

Eventually, I was finally able to say, "I thought you were working today?"

"I'm taking a morning break," she responded. "I tried to get back here as quickly as I could." Her mouth hung open, wanting to say more, but she ended up closing it. It was okay; she didn't have to say more. I knew what she wanted to say after what happened yesterday.

My stomach growled, and Mom heard it.

"I have some eggs, bacon, and toast cooking. Why don't you help yourself to some?"

I nodded and moved to the kitchen. "Where's Dad?" I asked her as I opened a cabinet and grabbed a plate.

"Well, you know," she started. "There's still a lot of bodies that need to go into the ground, and since it's been warm the past couple of days, the ground is going to thaw."

"But I thought he worked his hours for this week?" I asked.

Mom sighed. "You know your dad, always working."

Always working so he can try to get away from us, I thought, but didn't say aloud.

"Don't forget that there's going to be a memorial service at the church tonight," she said.

I nodded.

"And you need to look nice there, out of respect."

I nodded again. I didn't have to ask about what clothes I should wear. "Nice" always meant a dress, preferably one that didn't have bright colors and didn't attract too much attention.

"We need to bring a dish there. The church is going to distribute them among the people who lost loved ones."

"Mmmhmm."

"I thought it would do you some good to get out of the house today. Maybe go down to John's and pick up some things for a casserole?"

"Do you think Dad would be happy with that?"

She pursed her lips together before saying, "If he says anything, I'll tell him I sent you out, but you need to be on your best behavior. I shouldn't have to tell you that, but you know what I mean."

"I need to go look after the plants," I said as I got up, having barely touched my food.

"No, stay a bit," Mom said and gestured for me to take a seat. I sat back down, cutting up my eggs with my fork so she couldn't see the heat rising into my face. *Can't she just let me go?* I thought. I put a piece of the egg into my mouth. The yolk burst and I swallowed it down.

"How's everyone holding up at school?"

"They're okay."

Mom sighed. "I suppose that's all anyone can be doing right now, is okay." She grabbed onto her mug and held it up like she was about to take a sip of coffee, but it hovered before her lips. "You know, the ladies at the hotel are becoming so forgetful with everything. Yesterday, Sharon told me she had already cleaned a room and that I didn't have to worry about a thing. Well, when I got in there, the sheets were on the ground, fingerprints on the windows, and toothpaste in the sink." She laughed, and I gave her a weak smile. "Now, I don't know if they lost someone in the tragedy. They don't talk about such things; God help them if they did, but bless their hearts, it seems that some of their minds fell along with that bridge."

I nodded while taking a bite of my bacon.

"Now, how are the teachers doing? How's Mrs. Johnson?'

I thought it would be one more story for Mom to tell the other cleaners, and Mrs. Johnson doesn't need everyone to know about her breakdown.

Instead, I said, "She's holding up," and then, because it was such a short response and Mom always complained about short responses, I added, "She seems sad, but that's understandable."

"Oh, bless her heart. Do you know how long they were married?'

I shook my head.

Mom grimaced and leaned back in her chair. "I could not imagine something like that happening to you or your father. I don't know what I would do." She took a sip of her coffee while staring at the wall. I stared down at my plate as I gathered the remaining bits of eggs and bacon onto my fork and scooped them into my mouth.

"Well, luckily, we won't have to worry about that for a long time," she said.

I nodded and wiped my mouth on a napkin. "Are you going back in for work today?" Mom usually worked long shifts at the hotel during the weekends because so many of the ladies had young children to take care of back home and wanted to give their babysitters most of the weekends off.

"Yes, in about an hour or so," she said. "I think you'll have to meet us at the church unless Dad comes home early."

"Okay," I said. I picked up my plate and fork and took them to the sink, where I rinsed them off. "I'm going to take care of the plants."

"Okay."

~8~

As I walked across the dirt floor in the basement, clouds of dust formed around me. A musty smell hung in the air. I tugged on a cord in the center of the room, and the light bulb swayed, casting shadows across the gray walls.

I followed the light to see the natural light coming from the high windows on the left side of the room. Underneath the windows lay rows of plants, their leaves barely sprouting from the dirt they had been planted in only a couple of weeks before.

I picked up the tin watering can and turned on the spout beside it. Water with flakes of dirt in it poured from its source, and it smelled like pennies. When it was full, I used both hands to drag it to the first plant and began pouring the water across the rows.

As I poured, my gaze continued to linger towards the windows. *Look down,* I reminded myself, *you don't want to drown the plants.* But I couldn't help looking back up at the window.

Something moved across from the window, near the woods. I thought it was nothing more than a bag or a piece of paper, but as I continued to stare at it, water still dripping from the tin, the movement was distinctly animalistic.

It was teetering from one foot to the other.

It was so far away, but I knew it was taller than me. It stood up on its hind legs and had two golden lines curling around its head. Were those horns?

So far away, but I felt it looking directly back at me.

It's just an animal, I tried to convince myself. *Leave it alone.*

Something wet settled at my feet. I looked down and saw the water spilling over the plants onto the floor around me.

"Shit." I took the tin away and started trying to pour the water out without damaging the plants to keep them from drowning.

~9~

In my room, I waited to hear mom leave before I moved to my dresser. I rummaged through it until I pulled out my bell-bottom jeans and an orange and white flower shirt to wear. I took off my clothes and slipped them on. The shirt was wrinkled, but it would have to do. *I'm just going out to pick up groceries; I'm not trying to impress anyone*, I told myself.

I slipped on a pair of boots and walked downstairs. On the table in the foyer, Mom had laid out two ten-dollar bills next to the bowl where we kept our keys. I grabbed the money and my car keys, saying a quick prayer to whoever was listening that the warmer weather would allow my car to turn on – which it so preferred not to do during the winter. Then, I opened the door and stepped outside.

~10~

As I approached town, I saw the buildings scattered around each side of the road. Susie's Sewing, with its pink window frames and sign with letters made out of sewing stitches. Molly's Antiques, whose building had a broken window on the second floor. It had been like that for as long as I could remember. The steeple from St. Andrew's Church stuck out; I could see it from miles away.

I drove past the store that had been my favorite when I was a child, "The Toybox." A faint smile appeared across my face when I saw that the statues of building blocks were still outside the store. I sustained my first major injury after I had tried to climb those blocks when I was three. I fell off, and scraped my knee. My young mind thought I had broken all of my bones.

I could be happy here, I thought. At least, I tried to imagine myself five, even ten, or twenty years from now, living here, taking weekend trips with money from my savings, and going to college. Maybe Marshall, like Ellen. That way, I could be close if Mom or Dad ever needed me. I would have to get a job. *I should be getting one for this summer*, I thought. *How about John's?* I laughed when I thought about that.

The laughter died on my lips when I remembered last September. One of the few times – of which I could count on a single hand – that my mom had ever raised her voice at me.

"Fine, go to college!" She said when I brought it up at the start of my senior year. "But we don't have the money to pay for it! You won't be able to get a place of your own with all the debt you'll be in, so you'll come back here. All roads lead back to this house. Don't you think your father and I know that more than anyone else?"

She was right. By trying to change my life, I would end up

right back at the place I was trying to walk away from. But even if they were true, those thoughts didn't make the ache go away. With the aching, came the guilt.

I always wanted to blame Mom and Dad first. They could sell the house and move into a smaller, cheaper place. With the money from the sale, I could start college, and then I could get a job to continue paying for my education. But the house was their home as much as it was mine. If they weren't going to leave it, I wouldn't leave them. I would stay there as long as I needed to, as long as they needed me.

A lump burned at the back of my throat. I swallowed it down and tried to think about the sign in front of me. The wooden "John's Groceries" sign creaked on its rusty hinges in the breeze. I pulled into the parking lot and parked the car in front of the store. There were only two other cars there.

I got out, ensured the car was locked, and stepped inside. A country song played over the speakers. I walked over to the buggies and pulled one out. During the summer, the local produce was always displayed front and center for anyone who walked into the store. But during the winter, there wasn't much local produce to be found, so John displayed handmade items from small businesses. Today it was soaps and lotions. I picked up one of the bars – Roses and Lavender – and smelled it. The scent was sweet, and bits of rose petals and lavender blossoms peeked out from the bar.

Focus, I reminded myself and pushed the buggy down the aisle towards the back of the store, where John kept all of the frozen groceries. I opened the fridge, grabbed some cheese, milk, and eggs, and put them in the basket. I then moved down to an aisle with sauce and noodles. A rumbling came from the aisle beside me as if someone was moving around bags and boxes. I almost ignored it until I heard them talking.

"Have you heard about Matthew?"

"Oh no, don't tell me something else has happened to him. That poor man has had too much bad luck recently."

The voices sounded older, but I couldn't recognize them. I pushed the buggy slowly along to the cash register.

"I know, and I don't know anything for sure. He's been keeping to himself a lot recently. He won't even say hello to his neighbors when they stop by, but nobody has seen him leave the house. They're afraid he's going to starve up there if he doesn't get some food soon."

"Well, he's a grown man; he knows how to take care of himself."

"I know, that's what I told Mary, except she thinks that there might be something wrong with him," she whispered the last part. "Ever since the bridge collapsed, she's been woken up twice by him screaming outside in the night, telling some sort of devil creature to get off his lawn."

"Oh, my word."

I didn't catch the rest as I pushed the buggy to the register. John was working today. The laugh lines around his eyes stood out like carvings on a tree when he saw me and smiled.

"Alissa! I haven't seen you in a long time. How have you been?" He asked. I returned the smile and started putting my things onto the countertop.

"I'm holding up," I said. "How about you?"

"About the same. I suppose that's all we can manage to be doing right now."

I nodded and was reminded of my mom's statement from breakfast, and then in my mind, I was back in the basement, watering the flowers and seeing the horns. When I blinked, I saw red on the back of my eyelids. I felt the house shuddering under the creature's wings and had to shake off the chills across my shoulders.

The beeping register brought me back to reality.

I watched John's wrinkled hands pass the items into the bag.

How long had he owned this store? Perhaps he owned it before I was even born, and then a thought occurred to me.

"You've lived here a long time, haven't you?" I asked him.

"All my life."

"Have you ever seen anything strange in the woods?" I asked the question like it was nothing more than simple, innocent curiosity, but John stopped passing the items into a bag and stared at me.

"What do you mean?"

I wrung my hands together. "I don't know. Anything strange or unusual that shouldn't be in the forests? Like a creature with horns or red eyes?"

There was a moment of silence before John started laughing. Tears formed in the corners of my eyes. I blinked them back and tried to force a smile.

"You need to stop reading those scary books," he said. "Kids your age are obsessed with them. They always ask me if I have any in stock every time they come in here. Well, let me tell you something, those novels can't do you any good with you being out there in the woods and all that. What you're describing sounds like nothing but West Virginia folklore to me, and folklore is only stories."

A strained laugh tumbled from my lips. "You're right. I was only kidding with you," I remarked and handed John the money.

He took it, and then I grabbed onto the bags and put them in my buggy

"Thank you," I said.

"Alright. See you soon, and stay away from those scary stories."

I nodded in his direction and walked out of the store to my car. *West Virginia folklore*, I thought to myself as I unloaded the groceries into the back of my car and laughed. He was right. *Those Mothman stories the kids at school are saying are getting to me. God, am I that sensitive?*

I finished unloading the groceries and returned the buggy to the store. When it was in its place, I stopped and looked around, turning to face the other side of the street across from the grocery store.

There was a dying store: Molly's Antiques. Some of the windows were broken, and the paint that made up the lettering on the signs was peeled away, revealing the brown, rotting wood underneath. The "Open" sign hung at a crooked angle on the door.

I walked towards it, waiting for the cars to pass so I could cross the street. When I reached it, the door creaked open against my hand. Dust floated around me.

"Well, hello there," a mellow voice said. Her gray hair was piled on top of her head in a bun, and she wore a quilted skirt and a red sweater.

"Hello."

"I'm Molly, and you are?"

"Alissa."

"Ah, yes. Alissa Lee; I remember you. Well, look at you now; you're all grown up. You and your folks used to visit here when you were a little thing."

"Really? I don't remember."

"Oh, well, you were young. You should come by more often. We don't get a lot of people here anymore."

I nodded. It felt silly to do that, but she stared directly at me. I felt like I needed to do something.

"Are you looking for anything in particular?'

"No. I was just going to look around for a bit."

"Okay. Let me know if you need anything." She gave me a smile that took up her whole face and made her eyes close before she walked away and through a door in the back of the room.

There was a bookcase beside me that I started to glance over. On the shelves, there were stacks of gray photographs with yellow corners. Candle snuffers and boxes of mittens and hats were stacked near one another. Next to the bookcase was a clothing rack that held skirts and cardigans. They looked like they were handmade, and there was something comforting about that. I walked forward, and a white light of pain shot up through my toe. I gripped onto a nearby table and grabbed my foot with my other hand. My lips pursed together.

Right where I had meant to walk was a crate of books.

I placed my foot back on the ground, wincing as my big toe touched the floor, and pulled the crate up and onto the table. As I peered into it, I saw that all of the spines on the books were broken, and some of the letters were faded.

I shuffled through all of them. Most were romance novels, whose covers showed bare-chested men rescuing damsels in distress. I pushed those to the side. Others were works by Aristotle and Voltaire. I picked up one by Aristotle. As I turned the pages without reading any of the words, I felt a hollowness crawl up the sides of my stomach.

These are the types of books the people at school would read in college next year. Well, not all of them, but some of them. I would've read them, too, and had discussions about them. I wouldn't have to spend my days taking care of the plants and listening to my parents worry about money. It would be different, and it would be nice.

I really shouldn't be thinking about these things, I thought. *They'll just make me more upset.* I almost put the crate back underneath the table, but then I saw a little book tucked away at the bottom. I pulled it out.

Appalachian Folk Tales and Superstitions, the title read. There was a picture of Bigfoot on the cover. That made me smile. I would've laughed if it weren't so quiet in the shop.

"Well, John, I guess I'm not one to keep my promises," I said underneath my breath. I opened the cover of the book. $3 was written in pencil on the inside of the cover. I picked up the first Aristotle book in the pile. It was two dollars.

I walked up to the checkout desk and rang the bell on it. Molly came out of the back room, wiping her hands on her skirt and smiling.

"Alright, did you find everything okay?"

"Yes," I said as I handed her five dollars and a couple of quarters.

~11~

I drove past the curves that welcomed me onto Whispering Way, to the end of the street, where I pulled into our driveway. My ears were ringing as I got the groceries out of the trunk and carried them to the front porch, where I fumbled with the keys to unlock the door. There was pressure building in my nose, so I could only breathe out of my mouth.

I walked to the kitchen and set the noodles and sauce on the countertop and the bag of cold items in the fridge. Nausea clawed at the corners of my stomach and crept up my throat. I tried to swallow it back.

Should I lie down? I thought to myself, but upon staring out through the kitchen window and seeing the sun glisten on the grass, I thought a walk would do me good.

The sunlight had been deceiving, though, because heavy gray clouds took up the skies once I was on the road. The sun tried to fight through them and occasionally did, but the clouds would block its light after a moment of triumph. I had barely walked past my house when I heard a voice call after me.

"Hey, Alissa." The voice yelled, and I turned to where it was coming from.

Jenny stood on her front porch. Her apron - marked with flour - covered most of the sweater and pants she was wearing. She waved for me to come closer.

"Hey, sweetheart, what are you doing?" She asked.

"I was just going to go on a walk," I responded.

"Oh no, you don't want to do that. It's about to storm something awful out here." She saw me start to frown and added, "Why don't you come in and help me bake some cookies for the memorial tonight?"

I thought about the ingredients for a casserole I had left in my house, and then I thought about the smell of cookies filling a room. I told her I would help her out.

"Well, come on in before it starts storming," she said and held the door open for me. I walked in.

~12~

Jenny's house hadn't changed much since the last time I had been inside it in middle school. The old burgundy couch in the living room still had blankets tossed over it to cover the stains from spilled drinks and food. Jenny had let her girls eat in the living room when they were young – a point I had argued with my mom about after she told me I wasn't allowed to.

But the kitchen had changed. Flour spewed across the yellow countertops and left faint impressions on the tiled floor. Bits of dough clumped around the baking paper that held globs of unbaked cookies.

"I know what it looks like," Jenny started, but I stopped her.

"No, I know, it's a part of the creative process." She smiled at me. I returned the smile, and for the first time in a long time, it felt genuine on my face.

"And do you know what helps the creative process?"

I shook my head.

"Some music, of course." She turned to face the countertop, and, as she did so, I saw the outline of a teal, portable radio on the countertop.

"Do, wah, diddy, diddy, dum, diddy do," she sang along as it started. I laughed and then joined in with her. "There she goes, just a-walkin' down the street."

~13~

The house smelled incredible when the cookies finally came out of the oven. After they had finished cooling, we grabbed one each and sat at the table with glasses of milk to drink with them. The rain poured around us. A mixture of hail and sleet from what I could see outside Jenny's kitchen window.

"Oh, I wonder if they'll cancel the memorial service? Homemade cookies are never as good the next day."

"Are you kidding? These cookies are amazing! I don't think anyone would dare to state that the town's greatest baker is falling short on her baking skills?"

Jenny gave a soft smile. "My baking is one of the only good things I have going in this town, I suppose."

I fell silent and stared at my glass of milk before deciding that I should take a sip from it to look less awkward.

"It's okay, dear," she said. "My views are my own, and I wouldn't change them for the world. They helped me raise two great young girls. Now, I've seen some of the kids at your school, and I think that some parents teaching their kids acceptance would do them a world of good. It's sad to think that acceptance is a progressive view, but that's the way this town works."

"The town needs to catch up," I said.

Jenny patted me on the shoulder.

"Speaking of Amelia and Ellen, where are they?"

Jenny leaned back in her chair. "Is it bad to say, 'how should I know?'" We both laughed at that. Jenny dabbed at the corners of her eyes before she started again. "Ellen's back at college, so I really don't know where she is. She could be in her dorm or out partying or whatever, and then Amelia is supposed to be at John's. Now, I will be highly pissed if she isn't there because she's supposed to bring us back something to eat, since she wasn't happy with what I had here." The statement lost all of its seriousness when Jenny's smile only grew larger on her face. "Oh, you know people tell me how I should be stricter on my girls, but they're young girls. They're going to go out and party and do stuff that young people do, regardless of whether I had those strict rules or not. The important thing to me is that they know that this house is always a safe place, and they can return here whenever they want or need to."

"I wish you were my mom," I remarked, and I didn't realize how serious the statement was until Jenny's smile fell.

"Oh, honey, you know this is always a safe place for you too."

I nodded. Tears were welling in the corners of my eyes. *Why the hell am I so sensitive?* I thought to myself.

"Thank you so much for the cookies," I said, not quite being able to make eye contact with Jenny. "But I should be heading back now. My mom will be home any minute, and I have to get ready."

Jenny nodded. "Let me drive you back."

"No, don't be silly. It's less than a five-minute walk away."

Jenny turned down her chin and gave her serious eyes – the ones that always made her look like she was glaring. "I don't care how short of a walk it is; I am not going to let you walk out in this weather."

"I'll run. It will barely even get to me."

Jenny sighed. "Well then, at least let me give you an umbrella."

~14~

With Jenny's umbrella, I started on my way back home. I felt her watching me as I tried to push past the sharp, needle-like rain coming at me on all sides.

Why didn't you let Jenny drive you? I thought to myself, followed by the thought of, *I didn't want her to waste gas.*

She wouldn't have wasted any gas. No, you just didn't want her to ask about your home life, and you were afraid you would end up spilling the beans about the blue eyeshadow.

I shoved that thought back down until it became nothing more than a pit in my stomach. Amid the sounds of the rain pelting around me, I heard the breaking of branches. It was loud enough for me to look at my feet, wondering if I had just stepped onto glass or a wooden board and had broken it. There was nothing but the road underneath me.

I thought it could be an animal and started walking a bit faster. All the while, I looked around, making sure that something else wasn't outside. *What could be outside in this weather?* A voice taunted me in the back of my head. *Your scary creatures?*

It could be a deer, I thought, and the voice responded to my thoughts.

A deer wouldn't be out in this weather.

I kept my eyes on my house, where it was warm, and I could take a hot shower and get ready. But my eyes wandered to the forest around my house.

Standing in front of a tree was a creature covered in white fur. It stood on its hind legs, and its golden horns wrapped around its head. Its bloodshot eyes stood out in the storm, and it made black spots dance around my vision.

A branch broke.

It stepped forward.

I tried to move, but my muscles strained against my effort. Tears burned in the backs of my eyes.

It opened its mouth. A long, pink tongue slithered out against its brown, jagged teeth. It screeched at the sky.

I pushed my body forward.

Branches broke around me. My breaths burned in my chest. Darkness edged at the corners of my vision and made the world pulse around me until I could hardly see anything.

A stumble was all it took for me to fall to the ground.

When it screamed, I screamed too. A hollow, guttural sound mixed with my own.

I turned around and tried to push myself onto my hands and feet. Ahead of me, a shadow loomed.

It was large with wings and piercing red eyes. It beat its wings against the sky, and my hair wrapped around my face in the wind. The wind and the screams of the creature brought a ringing to my ears. Pinpricks of pain dotted their way across my arms and legs. Still, I pushed myself up and forward.

Its wings beat back. I nearly fell to the ground again, but I held myself up.

My house was so close. *I should have never left.*

And then, a low rumbling and bright lights made me stay in my place.

"Alissa, what in God's name—"

"Mom," I ran and tried to wrap my arms around her, but she grabbed my shoulders and held me there. All the while, she was searching my face.

"What has gotten into you, child?"

I tried to open my mouth to tell her something – everything – but I was shaking so badly. My teeth chattered, and I couldn't get my lips to stop quivering.

Mom pursed her lips together before saying, "Come on, let's

get in the car. We need to pick up your father." She sighed, staring at me, and added, "I have a coat in the back. You can put that over yourself unless you want to go inside and get new clothes?"

I shook my head, seeing red against my closed eyelids with every blink, and walked over to ride shotgun.

~15~

It wasn't until we passed the sign that said "Whispering Way" that I could finally hold onto my breaths and keep myself from shaking. Mom, having been silent up until this point, noticed the change.

"Are you going to tell me what's going on with you, or are we going to have to take you to a doctor? It's going to cost more money than we've got, but I don't mind spending it if we can figure out what's getting you all riled up. And it's not just today; you've been acting strange all week."

"I don't know what it is, Mom," I said, and my voice faltered on the syllables. I waited for her to laugh or say something like, "You and me both," but she remained silent.

"I've been seeing these things, these creatures in the woods, and I know they're not real. At least, I don't think they are. Maybe those stories the kids at school are telling are getting to me, but I didn't think I was that sensitive. Maybe I am that sensitive. You know, I've always gotta cry when someone else cries, and I just want to cry all the time now because I don't know what's happening, and—"

"What stories?" My mom asked, cutting me off.

I sighed and looked out the window because I didn't want to see her expression as I told her.

"They're all so stupid and so immature. They only started telling them after the bridge collapsed because of some stupid joke or because they wanted attention. I don't know—"

"What stories?"

"About the Mothman."

I waited for my mom to laugh again. The rain pelted against the car, and the windshield wipers screeched as they went back and forth and back and forth and back and forth.

But she never laughed. Instead, she said, "You think you're seeing the Mothman?"

"I don't know," I mumbled, and the tears were falling again, and the only thing that could come from my mouth were whimpers. We pulled into a parking lot, and I saw the tombstones around me.

Mom sighed and said, "I'm going to get your dad. We'll talk about this when we get back home. Can you stay in the car?"

I nodded. Mom looked at my face and pursed her lips together again.

"Okay," she said. "I'll be back in less than two minutes. Just stay here, okay?"

I nodded again because I couldn't say anything. My lips were quivering, and I felt a burning at the back of my throat. I turned away from her. She reached up a hand and patted me on the shoulder, which for some reason, made me cry harder. She opened the door and got out of the car into the rain.

I watched the raindrops chase each other on the windshield. There was an ache spreading around my head, and it started to make my mind go numb again. I tried not to look at my reflection; I just stared at the droplets.

A scream erupted around me, and I broke out of my trance.

I waited, for each heartbeat of a second, I waited. *Was my mind playing tricks on me?* I thought, followed by, *Great, I'm hearing things now. They're going to send me to an asylum for sure.*

My thoughts were broken when I heard another scream.

I fumbled at the door. My pulse was pushing against my skin, and my hands were shaking again.

The rain pelted me when I stood outside. It was cold and stung.

"Help!" The scream called out, and I ran towards it. There was a shadow ahead of me. He stood with his back hunched over; hands hung limply at his sides.

I didn't stop running until I reached him.

"Who are you?" He asked, but I didn't answer it because, when I saw what he had seen, I started screaming too.

Six feet deep, that was how far my father had dug. He had done it so many times up to this point that he probably didn't have to measure it anymore.

At the bottom of the hole, mixing with the rainwater, was blood streaming from my father's head. His eyes stared back up at me, empty and lifeless.

"He wouldn't listen. He wanted to finish the job. The shovel. Oh, Sweet Jesus, the shovel. It sliced his head, like, like..."

Mom lay wrapped around him. Her hair - the same brown color I would see in the feathers underneath their pillows only three days later - curled around her pale skin like worms.

"...butter. Like a knife through butter. Oh, Sweet Jesus, oh, God. She wasn't supposed to — I tried. Oh God, please believe me, I tried!"

It was like she was kissing his forehead. So soft, so gentle, but it wasn't right. Not with the shovel inside her, a flap of skin on the side of her neck still caught on the metal. How would she ever talk again?

"She tried to help him. She pulled him up, but he slipped, slipped like everything else, and he dragged her along. She landed on the shovel. I tried to stop her. I tried to help. But the shovel, like a knife through but— I think I'm gonna be sick."

I leaned forward. *They have to get out. I have to pull them out.* My feet slid on the grave's edge when the man pulled me back.

"They have to get out! I have to pull them out!" I wailed. He held on tightly as I screamed and kicked at him.

The man let out a grunt before he said, "Not you too!"

~16~

"Tonight, we are remembering two individuals. Two members of our community, of our church, of our lives, but most importantly, two caring parents who passed in a tragedy," the pastor said. "May we all remember the lovely impacts that they left on all of our souls. Now, Miss Woolston, would you please join us all in a song of remembrance."

A girl, dressed in all black, walked up to the podium.

"Nearer my God to thee, nearer to thee," she sang. "Even though it be a cross that raiseth me. Still, all my song shall be, nearer my God to thee. Though like the wanderer the sun gone down. Darkness be over me, my rest a stone..."

~17~

After the funeral, I took the ashes outside. I heard someone trying to follow me, and Allison said, "No, she needs this moment."

I walked the entirety of the house, picking out handfuls of gray ashes and scattering them from the palm of my hand. They sank into the snow. My tears fell into my palms and stained the ashes until they turned the colors of shadows. The quiet hum of winter sang my parents to their forever sleep.

~18~

I sat on my knees and stared at the wall behind my headboard. I didn't know if I wanted to believe it or not. I think that was the real issue.

I traced the spindles of wood curling into one another on the wall, traveling along them as if they were a path. I followed it to the carved "X."

"Why?!" I screamed, my voice breaking apart as it became louder. "Why did you have to take them?" As I wiped the tears away, my faltering gaze fell on my nightstand, where the gas station bag lay. I crawled to it and opened it, revealing the blue eye shadow in its glass case.

"Fucking gorgeous," I whispered and took the eye shadow out.

~19~

Dad always had to finish the job. Mom always had to help him, whether he wanted it or not. When I crawled into my parents' bed, their spirits were still acting out on these habits.

The sunlight washed over their blankets and pillows. The doors to their closets were slightly open, and the air was stale. Everything was quiet and peaceful as if nothing had ever happened and nothing would ever happen. I removed the blankets and pillows first and held them in my hands. "I'll take them to Florida with me, with Aunt Allison," I whispered, a promise to myself.

From the corner of my vision, I saw something fall from one of the pillows. It was so fast; it couldn't have been more than a speck of dust. But I looked to the ground, and there it was. There were two of them. I held them in my hands. They were clumps of feathers, twined together, so they both made up separate spirals.

Their weight in my hands made me breathe easier, confirming that I knew what they were.

Death Crowns.

My blurry vision from the all-too-familiar tears forming once more made it difficult for me to see every detail of them. I sat on the edge of the bed and I held them and cried, the blue eyeshadow marking my hands. When I looked up and stared out the window, I saw my reflection.

The blue eye shadow trailed from my eyes, down my face, following the path my tears had created for them. I clutched the Death Crowns in my hands and ran out of the room. Aunt Allison called me from the kitchen, but I kept running until I was outside and on the street.

"Wait up, Alissa!" Aunt Allison yelled. My panting breaths mixed with my sobs, but my feet carried me to the end.

At the end of Whispering Way, there is a pile of rubble. There once was something there, as all piles of rubble once existed as something else. Now, nobody sees anything in it anymore. I crouched down and laid the Death Crowns on the pebbles. Then, I picked up a brick and placed it in front of me. I grabbed another brick and set it around the crowns.

"Alissa, what in God's name…"

I scooped up handfuls of gravel and scattered it around. As my hands began to sting in the winter air, I heard Allison's muffled cries around me, and I began to build a city.

ACKNOWLEDGMENTS

I would like to express my greatest appreciation to The Henlo Press. Through Chandler Haun and C.W. Phelps's guidance, I have been able to bring my stories to their greatest potentials. As a result, they have helped me to create a collection that I am proud of.

I would also like to thank Bob Harrison, who helped me edit my stories in their earliest forms.

The greatest of thanks to my friends and family. Without your love and support, Mumblings would have never happened. I love each and every one of you.

Thank you to Joel Carroll, Kody Christian, and Kaitlyn Taylor for the lovely art you created for my collection. You all are truly fantastic and incredible artists.

And thank you, reader, for taking a chance on my stories. I hope that some of them thrilled and scared you, while others touched your heart. Perhaps, in the best of circumstances, each story did both for you.

AN EXTRA SPECIAL THANK YOU

To our Kickstarter Backers,
Thank you for being the first to believe in this book. We couldn't
have done it without you and your generous support.

ABOUT THE AUTHOR

Caitlyn Pace is a horror and dark fiction writer. She resides in West Virginia, where she is often inspired by the folklore and ghost stories surrounding her state and the Appalachian region.
Keep updated with her through her Twitter @CaitlynPace02
or email her at
catilynpace02@gmail.com